GABE

LANTERN BEACH BLACKOUT: THE NEW
RECRUITS BOOK 4

CHRISTY BARRITT

COMPLETE BOOK LIST

Squeaky Clean Mysteries:

#1 Hazardous Duty

#2 Suspicious Minds

#2.5 It Came Upon a Midnight Crime (novella)

#3 Organized Grime

#4 Dirty Deeds

#5 The Scum of All Fears

#6 To Love, Honor and Perish

#7 Mucky Streak

#8 Foul Play

#9 Broom & Gloom

#10 Dust and Obey

#11 Thrill Squeaker

#11.5 Swept Away (novella)

#12 Cunning Attractions

Lantern Beach Romantic Suspense

Tides of Deception

Shadow of Intrigue

Storm of Doubt

Winds of Danger

Rains of Remorse

Torrents of Fear

Lantern Beach P.D.

On the Lookout

Attempt to Locate

First Degree Murder

Dead on Arrival

Plan of Action

Lantern Beach Escape

Afterglow (a novelette)

Lantern Beach Blackout

Dark Water

Safe Harbor

Ripple Effect

Rising Tide

Lantern Beach Guardians

Hide and Seek

The Good Girl

Suspense:
Imperfect
The Wrecking

Sweet Christmas Novella:
Home to Chestnut Grove

Standalone Romantic-Suspense:
Keeping Guard
The Last Target
Race Against Time
Ricochet
Key Witness
Lifeline
High-Stakes Holiday Reunion
Desperate Measures
Hidden Agenda
Mountain Hideaway
Dark Harbor
Shadow of Suspicion
The Baby Assignment
The Cradle Conspiracy
Trained to Defend
Mountain Survival

Nonfiction:

Characters in the Kitchen

Changed: True Stories of Finding God through Christian Music (out of print)

The Novel in Me: The Beginner's Guide to Writing and Publishing a Novel (out of print)

CHAPTER ONE

"YEAH, man, that sounds good. Let's plan the trip for Labor Day weekend." Gabe Michaels jogged down the road as he spoke to his friend through his earbuds.

"I'll see if I can get up with Mikey, and we'll make this happen." Brandon Banks' familiar voice filled the line.

Gabe frowned upon hearing Mikey's name. "I'm glad you mentioned Mikey. I've been trying to reach him, but he hasn't answered or called me back."

Brandon let out a grunt. "The last I heard he took a solo backpacking trip near Sedona. It was supposed to take a few weeks, one of those 'finding yourself' kind of deals."

Gabe could see their friend doing that. Mikey

was always looking for new adventures and avenues of self-discovery. "What you're telling me matches the timeline of when I started calling him. But I'll keep trying and hopefully get up with him in time for the trip."

"That sounds good. I look forward to catching up with everyone. It sounds like you and the rest of the guys have been having more fun than I have."

"You mean you don't like being a car salesman?" As Gabe's lips curled up in a smile, he glanced around, scanning the beach houses on either side of him, along with the ditches lining the road, where reeds shot up from the stagnant water.

Noticing details and staying on guard was a side effect of his job, one he couldn't seem to shrug—not that he'd want to.

"I'm pretty sure I don't even have to give you an answer to that."

Gabe chuckled. From the moment Brandon announced he'd taken the job, Gabe had known his friend would be miserable. He was a tactical guy who was always ready for adventure. Making sales pitches about the latest model cars with all the bells and whistles? Gabe was surprised his friend had lasted this long.

"I was just offered another job, however,"

Brandon said. "With a startup private security group called Dagger. Ever heard of them?"

"Can't say I have. You going to take it?"

"Probably not. I need a little break right now."

"Understood," Gabe said. "I'll be in touch."

He ended the call and continued jogging down the stretch of highway that cut through the center of the narrow island of Lantern Beach. The early morning sun beat down on him, and sweat covered his back. It was only eight o'clock, but the day was going to be another hot one. August was like that.

Gabe had been trying to organize a camping trip with several former SEAL buddies. He and his team-mates with the private security firm Blackout had been especially busy lately, and getting away would be good for all of them.

That's why Gabe wanted to plan a reunion. He was hoping they could all meet out in the Shenandoah Mountains for a weekend together. Hiking. Rafting. Climbing. Biking. The works.

Gabe's feet continued to pound the pavement as he pushed himself forward. Jogging was his way of working out his tension. Thankfully, his week so far had been relatively stress-free.

As the thought went through his mind, a familiar ache pulsated in his shoulder.

People didn't come back from wars without any scars.

He'd been dealing with the pain for a while. He'd gone to physical therapy, trying to make it better. But nothing had worked, so now he simply tried to live with the discomfort.

But what others didn't realize was that most of the scars SEALs came back with—the deepest ones—were unseen.

Gabe hit a button on his phone and strands of "Livin' on a Prayer" by Bon Jovi began playing. He loved eighties rock more than he would admit. He sang along with the chorus as he kept a steady pace, making sure the earbuds didn't block out all the ambient noises around him.

It wouldn't be safe. Especially not on a narrow two-lane road like this.

As he sang, he thought about Mikey again. That was a long hiking trip he'd embarked on. And to go alone? Mikey had always had a bit of a crazy streak to him. So, in some ways, imagining him on such an extended adventure wasn't surprising.

Gabe heard a car approaching and glanced behind him. He saw a blue sedan coming his way and moved to the prickly grass on the side of the road.

Probably a family of vacationers coming to the island for a week of adventure.

He wondered what it would be like to be that carefree.

Growing up, he'd dreamed about having a family who loved each other enough that they wanted to spend time together on trips. Unfortunately, his family hadn't been like that.

Gabe glanced back again to see how close the oncoming car was.

As he did, his eyes widened.

The sedan was riding the edge of the road—and getting nearer by the second.

It almost seemed like the driver pressed harder on the accelerator.

Didn't the person behind the wheel see Gabe? Or was the driver on the phone and not paying attention?

Gabe turned toward the car and waved his hands in the air, trying to catch the motorist's eye.

But the car continued to charge forward, going faster and faster.

Gabe squinted as he tried to see through the tinted windows, as he tried to get a glimpse of who was behind the wheel.

All he knew was that the car barreled toward him.

He waved again, desperate to get the driver's attention.

It didn't slow.

Gabe glanced at the ditch on the side of the road. The crevice was full of brown, murky water from a recent thunderstorm. Reeds grew around the side of it, and it wouldn't surprise him if water moccasins lingered amid the tall grass.

But he had to do something.

Gabe made a split-second decision.

Just as something brushed his leg, he dove off the road.

But it was too late.

Pain ripped through his side.

He'd been hit.

SEATED behind the clinic's front desk, Dr. Autumn Spenser quickly reviewed a call that had just come in.

A hit-and-run with injuries.

As she studied the notes, the doors burst open and paramedics whisked someone inside.

She placed her electronic tablet on the desk and rushed toward the man on the stretcher.

Her eyes widened when she saw his face.

She'd seen this man before. She was nearly certain he worked for Blackout.

He was conscious, but an oxygen mask was strapped over his mouth. His shirt was ripped and bloody, as were his shorts and one leg. From the looks of his outfit, he'd been jogging.

"What happened?" Autumn glanced at one of the paramedics as he walked beside the gurney.

"Name is Gabe Michaels. Twenty-nine years old. He was jogging down the road when a car side-swiped him. He's lucky to be alive."

"Injuries?"

"Best we can tell, his left leg and side are scraped up pretty bad—partly from the car and partly from a stump hidden beneath the reeds along the ditch. His ribs took the worst of it."

"Anything broken?"

"Doesn't appear to be, but he seems to be in a lot of pain."

Her gaze lingered on Gabe as she tried to determine how best to proceed. She thought she could manage his injuries here at the clinic. More serious cases were sent to Raleigh for treatment.

"Let's get him into one of the examination rooms so I can check him out," Autumn said.

They wheeled him into a room down the hall. As the paramedics transferred him onto a bed, Autumn pulled on gloves.

The man murmured something beneath his oxygen mask, but Autumn couldn't make out his words.

She moved to his side, wondering if he was trying to tell her what hurt.

He pulled his mask down, and his haggard gaze locked onto hers. "Not . . . an . . . accident."

Autumn's eyes narrowed. "What?"

His face squeezed with pain, wrinkles creasing his brow and blood trickling from his lip. "This was . . . on purpose."

Was he saying someone had intentionally hit him with their vehicle?

Her heart pounded harder. As horrible as that sounded, it wasn't her job to investigate. No doubt, the police were working on that now.

Before she could respond, Gabe seemed to get a sudden burst of strength. He threw his legs off the bed, tugged at his IV, and tried to stand. "Need to . . . find him."

Autumn pushed him back down, realizing he

was currently not in his right mind. "You're not going anywhere, Mr. Michaels."

"No . . . time . . . for this."

He tried to push himself to his feet again, stronger than Autumn expected him to be in this condition. As he started to stumble forward, one of his hands went to his side. He let out a moan as his face grew paler.

When Autumn saw Gabe's expression pinch again, she instructed her nurse to give him a sedative and some pain reliever. She rattled off the drug names and dosages.

Autumn wouldn't be able to treat him in his current state. He was too agitated and not in a good frame of mind.

Nurse Hannah added the medication to his IV. As she did, Gabe's eyes closed and Autumn helped lower him back onto the bed.

"Tried . . . to . . . kill me," he muttered before going still.

Hannah pulled the oxygen mask back over his face as the medicine took effect.

It was just as well. Treating his injuries wasn't going to feel good.

An hour later, Gabe's wounds had been cleaned and bandaged, his lacerations had been sutured, and his bruised midsection had an ice pack on it to reduce swelling—thanks to a fractured rib.

Gabe was lucky. His injuries could have been much worse.

Autumn wiped a hand across her brow as she lingered in his room filling out paperwork.

Things were more exciting here on Lantern Beach than she'd thought they would be. When she'd come to the island a couple of months ago, she never pictured how busy she'd be.

But she wasn't complaining. If there were people here who needed medical help, then she was happy to offer her services.

"That was my favorite shirt," someone muttered behind her.

She turned and saw that Gabe was awake. After setting down her notes, she paced toward him.

"Come again?"

"That was my favorite T-shirt." He pulled down his oxygen mask and nodded toward a bag of his personal belongings on the table beside him.

His favorite T-shirt? *That* was what he was worried about right now? The fact that his Lantern Beach tee had been shredded and bloodied? That Autumn had to cut it off?

"I'm sure you can get a new one," she assured him.

"But that shirt made me an official Lantern Beach resident. That's what the mayor told me." His voice sounded gravelly. "You can't replace stuff like that."

"Oh, yeah? Well, I live in Lantern Beach, and I don't have a shirt like that. Does that mean I'm not official?"

"It means you're missing out."

She resisted a laugh and shook her head. This wasn't a conversation she'd expected to have, but now she needed to turn her thoughts back to the job at hand.

Gabe's smile faded. "Thank you for taking care of me."

"You're welcome." She studied his face as she tried to ascertain how he was doing.

The man was handsome, with light-brown hair, engaging blue eyes, and a strong build. He clearly worked out and had some impressively defined muscles beneath his scrapes and bruises.

"How are you feeling?" She studied his expression.

He shrugged. "I've been better. But I've been worse."

"Sounds about right. You're very lucky to be alive. Speaking of which . . . the police chief is waiting outside. She wants to take your statement. Do you remember what happened?"

His eyes narrowed. "I can tell you exactly what happened. Someone tried to kill me."

Autumn continued to study his face, but Gabe gave no indication he was joking. The words he'd said earlier . . . she'd thought he'd been delirious. But what if he wasn't?

"Tried to kill you?" she repeated. "Are you sure it just wasn't an accident? Someone not paying any attention to where they were going?"

"It was on purpose. I'm certain of it." His gaze remained unwavering.

Autumn didn't like the sound of that. "Well, you'll have to explain that to the police chief then."

"I will." He glanced at the clock hanging on the wall. "When can I leave?"

He'd just nearly been killed and all he was worried about was leaving? Interesting. "I want to keep you here for observation for a while longer. Why? Are you in a hurry to get somewhere?"

Gabe's eyes narrowed, and he glanced out the window. "I want to find out who did this to me."

The anger in his voice made her pause.

"Shouldn't you just leave that to the police? Especially considering your cracked rib."

"I'm not good at leaving my problems to other people."

Autumn could respect that, even though she also knew she should discourage this man from looking into the hit-and-run himself. However, if she remembered correctly, he was a former Navy SEAL. She doubted she'd be able to convince him to leave this alone.

As she heard a knock at the door, she looked up and saw the police chief standing there. Chief Cassidy Chambers had her blonde hair pulled back into a bun, and her growing belly let it be known she was expecting a baby in a few months.

Autumn had gotten to know the woman since she'd been in town and had always enjoyed speaking with Cassidy.

"Dr. Spenser, could I have a word with Gabe?" Chief Chambers asked.

Autumn stepped toward the door. "He's all yours. I hope you have better luck with him than I did."

"I let you off easy," Gabe called.

As Autumn walked away, she couldn't help but wonder why someone might purposefully hit Gabe. Was it an enemy from his past? Certainly he had his fair share, considering what he did for a living.

She supposed it didn't matter. She would mind her own business.

But she had to admit that she was curious.

CHAPTER TWO

"I'M TELLING YOU, it was on purpose." Gabe locked his gaze with the police chief's. He needed to get through to her. He could search for the person who did this himself, but having a team behind him was always helpful.

Besides, Cassidy's husband was one of the cofounders of Blackout, so Cassidy knew, better than anyone, the perils of this job.

Cassidy crossed her arms. "I try to keep abreast of everything going on at Blackout, but I have to admit that lately it's been a lot. Or maybe it's pregnancy brain. Is there anything you need to bring me up to date on?"

Gabe searched his mind for a good reason why

this might have happened. But he came up blank—at least blank of any specific threats.

"There's no telling why somebody might want to hurt me. But I'm telling you, if I hadn't dived out of the way when I did, I wouldn't be here right now."

"I understand." She frowned and rubbed her belly. "Can you describe the car?"

He closed his eyes and let his mind drift back in time. "It was a sedan. Dark blue with tinted windows. I'm not sure, but I feel like only one person was inside. I could only see shadows, however. If I had to guess, I think it was a Honda. A newer model. Not the biggest or the most compact but somewhere in between."

Cassidy took notes before nodding. "I'll look into it."

His mind continued to race. "I don't suppose anybody saw anything?"

"No one we've talked to yet. I'm glad that you're okay. I'll investigate and give it all I've got. I can promise you that."

"Thanks, Chief." Gabe knew she would. The woman had proven herself to be competent on more than one occasion.

She stepped back but paused. "Do you need a ride back to Blackout?"

That was a good question. He hadn't thought that far ahead. "I need to call Colton and let him know what happened."

"I already heard," a deep voice said from the hallway.

Gabe looked up and saw his boss standing in the doorway. "Word travels quick in a small town."

"You better believe it." Colton stepped inside and crossed his arms, an intense look in his eyes. "I can take it from here, Cassidy. Unless there's more you need from him."

"I think I've got everything. But I'll be in touch if I have more questions or any updates."

Colton stepped closer to Gabe's bed. "I'm glad you're doing okay."

Gabe scowled. He was really tired of hearing that. What he wanted to hear was, "I have a lead on who did this."

Colton nodded toward the door. "As soon as they give you the okay, let's get you out of here and find out who tried to run you over."

"Yeah, well, I'm not going to argue with that. This isn't exactly where I want to be." He touched the bandage at his side. This was going to hurt even worse in the morning.

Colton stared at him, something else in his gaze. What was his leader not telling him?

"What?" Gabe asked.

Colton paused and rubbed his jaw, almost as if he didn't want to continue but knew he had no choice. "As you know, two other SEALs from our squadron have died. Their deaths were tragic, but now I'm convinced that they were also connected."

He sucked in a breath. "Do you think they were murdered?"

A shadow passed through his gaze. "That's my suspicion. Rocco and I have talked about it numerous times, and we've been trying to uncover more."

"Who would be trying to kill us?" Gabe took a breath, the words sounding surreal even to his own ears. "Never mind. Scratch that. We have a long list of people we've made mad. But you really think that John Belching's and Quinn Deblois' deaths are connected?"

Colton nodded, the grim look remaining in his gaze. "Not only that, but I've been trying to get up with Mikey."

"I talked to Brandon. He said Mikey is supposedly hiking out in Sedona."

Colton's jaw visibly tightened. "That's what I

heard too."

"You don't think . . . ?" Gabe paused, not wanting to finish his statement.

But the theory in his mind took shape. And it made sense.

A lot of sense.

How could Gabe not have seen this earlier?

Was someone killing off men Gabe had worked with? John and Quinn hadn't been on his SEAL team, but they'd all worked together in some capacity.

Colton's gaze looked stormy. "I asked someone I know out in Arizona to look into Mikey's disappearance. He should be back by now, and I want answers. We need to figure out what's really going on—if anything."

"Yes, we do. If SEALs are being killed off . . ." He didn't finish his statement.

Colton stepped back. "You concentrate on getting better. When you're up for it, you can come back to work."

Gabe didn't need to be handled with kid gloves. As the youngest member of the team, he was constantly fighting to earn the other guys' respect. "I'll be up for it as soon as I leave this place."

A smile flickered through Colton's gaze. "I've

always liked your spirit, Junior."

Gabe scowled. He hated that nickname. But as the youngest of the group, he took the majority of the ribbing from the rest of the guys.

Nickname aside, they had a lot of work to do.

But, first, Gabe needed to be cleared by the pretty doctor so he could get out of here.

AUTUMN PAUSED OUTSIDE THE DOORWAY. She'd come back to get the electronic tablet she'd accidentally left in Gabe's examination room when she overheard the last part of that conversation.

Former SEAL team members were being killed?

Her heart pounded in her ears at the words.

She'd come to Lantern Beach to get away from trouble. When would she learn that wasn't a possibility? Trouble would follow her wherever she went. There was no skipping it or hiding from it. Not permanently at least.

Her cheeks flushed as Colton Locke stepped out the door and nodded to her. Autumn nodded back, trying to pretend like she hadn't heard anything. That she didn't know what was going on.

But the look in his eyes held a touch of warning.

She wasn't supposed to hear any of that.

"I'm going to grab some coffee," Colton muttered. "But I'll be back to pick him up as soon as you release him."

"We'll give you a call," Autumn said.

She stepped back into the room and noticed Gabe rubbing his shoulder.

Something about his motions made her pause. "Did you hurt your shoulder too?"

His eyes narrowed with discomfort as he continued to massage his shoulder. "No, just one of my many ailments."

"You have a lot, huh?"

He let out a quick chuckle. "You could say that. We all do."

Autumn paused by the foot of his bed and crossed her arms, his words causing curiosity to spike in her. "What do you mean?"

"I work for Blackout," he explained.

She resisted saying, "I know." Instead, she nodded.

"We're all former SEALs. The guys on my team .. . we all came back from one of our operations messed up. In the middle of one of our missions, enemy combatants sprayed some kind of gas on us. It's affected us each in different ways."

Autumn's curiosity spiked higher. "Tell me more."

"Rocco gets migraines. Axel's vision gets blurry. Beckett loses feeling in his hands. And my muscles ache. It's the gift that keeps giving."

Her mind raced as she collected and stored each fact. "Strange how this substance is having such different effects."

"Isn't it?" He shrugged and moved his hand from his shoulder, bringing it back down to his side.

"Have you ever talked to any government or military officials about this? Demanded answers?"

"The government will only tell you what they want you to know." Gabe's voice contained a touch of resentment or bitterness. Maybe both.

"If it was me, I'd be doing everything possible to find answers." These guys seemed like they'd do the same. Navy SEALs weren't the type to be walked on.

Gabe shrugged. "Yeah, well, I guess we've had other things to worry about."

"I see. We took a sample of your blood. I'd like to run some tests on it. See if there are any hits. Maybe something will show up. Blood pathogens were my specialty in medical school."

His eyes widened, almost as if he were impressed. "Is that right?"

"It is. I know . . . I'm *such* a nerd. While my friends were out socializing, I was in the lab trying to learn everything I could about the human body." Curiosity had been her best friend and worst enemy —now and then.

"A nerd is the last thing I'd call you." An unreadable emotion gleamed in his eyes.

Autumn felt her cheeks heat. How could someone so confident in her job and in every other area of her life feel self-conscious when it came to men?

Probably because the one man she'd trusted with her heart had crushed it.

She liked to focus on what she was good at. That's why she was more curious than ever about what exactly was going on with the Blackout team.

In fact, as soon as Autumn had the chance, she'd run Gabe's blood through some tests. Study it under a microscope. Maybe even consult with her former mentor.

Maybe she could provide Gabe with some answers.

Because sometimes answers could be the first step to healing and a peaceful future.

Autumn knew that all too well herself.

CHAPTER THREE

TWO HOURS LATER, the Blackout team convened at headquarters to discuss what had happened to Gabe earlier.

Gabe was the last to arrive. He strode into the room and carefully lowered himself into a chair at the conference table. More than his physical injuries bothered him. Anger simmered inside him over what had happened.

"You sure you're okay to be here, Junior?" Rocco Foster's British accent rang through the room as the team leader studied him. "We'd all understand if you wanted to take it easy for the rest of the day."

"You're not going to get rid of me that easily." Gabe had taken some pain medication, just as he'd promised. He'd be just fine. He would make sure of it.

Colton had given him a ride back to the campus. Gabe had kept his eyes open the entire drive for the sedan that had hit him. When they passed the spot where the collision had occurred, Gabe had flinched as he mentally relived the incident.

He really was lucky he wasn't in worse shape.

If he'd turned his music up, if he hadn't looked behind him, if he hadn't dived out of the way when he did, he might not be sitting here right now.

"Glad you're okay." Axel Hendrix turned toward him, his eyes glinting with amusement. "I heard your future wife treated you."

Gabe scowled. The first time he'd seen Dr. Spenser, he may have accidentally made a public declaration that he was going to marry her one day. Something about the woman had captured his thoughts right from the start.

The problem was, at that point, he'd never even spoken with her. He'd mostly just watched and admired her from a distance.

"I was just waiting for one of you to bring that up," Gabe muttered.

"Are you sure you didn't pay someone to run you

off the road so a certain doctor could treat you?" Beckett Jones' eyes gleamed with humor.

"Ha, ha. Very funny guys." Gabe crossed his arms and leaned back.

He wanted to be mad. But he couldn't be. He'd done this to himself.

From the first moment he'd seen Autumn, he was taken with the woman's cool confidence and undeniable beauty. Her long auburn hair fell in waves to her shoulders. Freckles scattered across her cheeks and nose. Her green eyes were intelligent and perceptive.

"As much as I'd like to keep this lighthearted and enlightening conversation going, we do have other more pressing matters to discuss—matters slightly more important than Gabe's love life." Colton gave them all a pointed look.

"I concur." The amusement left Axel's eyes as he sobered. "So, you really think today's incident was another attempt to take down a member of our SEAL team?"

Colton turned to address everyone at the table. "I do. There's a very clear pattern developing here. We can't ignore it anymore."

"Why would someone want to take us out?"

Rocco narrowed his eyes, a new somberness capturing his features. "And who?"

"There are too many possibilities to list," Axel said. "In our line of work, we've made a lot of people mad."

"We all know that we have a lot of enemies," Colton continued. "We've taken out insurgents. Brought down terrorists. Foiled plots to destroy entire cities. If we started making a list today, we could still be here tomorrow morning and not have an exhaustive list."

"I haven't received any threats," Rocco said. "Has anyone else?"

Everyone shook their heads.

"Then we need to start trying to narrow this down to the most likely suspects." Colton's gaze met his team members. "And we need to do that now."

AUTUMN LEFT the hospital that evening after a long day at work.

Mostly small stuff had kept her busy. Stitches for someone who'd stepped on some glass on the beach. A quick check on someone who'd swallowed some ocean water. Medication for an asthma flare-up.

When she hadn't been working with her patients, she'd escaped to the small lab at the Lantern Beach Medical Clinic and studied Gabe Michaels' blood samples.

She was going to send them to the state lab for further testing. But, in the meantime, she'd sent a sample to her former professor and mentor, Dr. Leroy Johnson, a man who specialized in blood pathogens. She hoped he might have some answers for her. He was the most brilliant man she knew.

He hadn't responded to her message yet, but Autumn felt certain that he would soon. He was always very responsive.

By the time Autumn pulled up to the small cottage she rented, darkness filled the sky. She hoped to buy her own place within the next few years—as soon as she paid off her medical school loans. She would like to have made it through school without any debt, but that hadn't been possible.

Instead, she was grateful for the small place she had now. The cottage wasn't on the water—even though she dreamed about having a place there one day. She wanted to wake up to the scent of the sea, to watch the waves attack then retreat, to see dolphins playing outside her window.

She climbed the stairs and stepped into the

small one-story space with two bedrooms and flipped on the light in her living area. After placing her purse on the table by the door, she stepped farther into her cottage.

The owner had given her permission to fix the place up, so that was what she did in her free time. She'd already painted the walls a pleasant greenish-blue color that reminded her of the early morning sky on a clear day.

Next, she was going to paint the kitchen cabinets white instead of the orange-colored oak they currently were.

But right now, all she could think about was hopping in the shower and washing away today's grime.

She enjoyed treating patients at the clinic. But people were usually surprised to learn that she was a bit of a germaphobe. She loved nothing more than a long, hot shower at the end of the day.

She detoured into her bedroom and flipped on the light switch so she could grab her pajamas.

But nothing happened. The room remained dark.

Strange. Had her lightbulb burnt out?

That must be it since the electricity worked in the rest of the house.

She'd have to head back into her utility closet and see if she had any extra lightbulbs there.

After she took her shower.

She felt fairly certain she'd left her pajamas on the end of her bed. She would creep forward and grab them.

But as she stepped farther into the dark space, she heard a noise beside her.

Her heart rate quickened.

She started to turn, to see what the noise was.

Before she could, a man grabbed her. One strong arm stretched across the front of her and held her in place. His other hand pressed into her mouth, muting her scream.

She fought the intruder. Jerked. Kicked. Did everything she could think of to get away.

But it was no use. He was too strong.

"You don't know what you've done," the man growled.

CHAPTER FOUR

GABE GRASPED the shirt in his hand as he strode toward Autumn Spenser's doorway.

He knew this was risky.

That his presence could be taken the wrong way.

He was going to give this a shot anyway.

As he took the first step onto her deck, a crash came from inside Autumn's place, followed by a scream.

He dropped the shirt and darted up the stairs, taking them two steps at a time.

Without knocking, he burst inside the doctor's home.

Where had the sound come from?

Footsteps pounded at the back of the house.

He darted toward the noise. As he paused at the

first doorway, he looked over and spotted Autumn lying on the floor, a hand at her throat.

He rushed toward her, concern pulsing through him. "Are you okay?"

She nodded and pointed toward the hallway, her eyes dazed and fearful.

Someone had done this to her, he realized.

Someone who'd just run.

"Call the police!" he yelled before sprinting back into the hallway. As he paused, a door slammed at the back of the house.

Autumn's attacker was trying to get away.

He couldn't let that happen.

He tore down the hallway, trying to catch the man. But the pain in his side slowed him down, his earlier accident handicapping him.

He pressed forward anyway, determined not to let someone get away with this.

As he reached the back of the hallway, he spotted another door there. A back exit.

He threw it open and quickly surveyed the area in front of him.

A figure in black darted down the road.

As Gabe took off after him, another burst of pain ripped through his side. He flinched but ignored the soreness.

Right now, he needed to catch this guy.

As he reached the bottom step, a car door opened and tires squealed.

Gabe paused and watched as taillights pulled onto the highway.

There was no way he was going to catch this guy now.

At least Gabe had shown up when he did and had been able to run the intruder off.

But he still had a lot of questions.

———

AUTUMN STOOD at the back door watching the taillights disappear.

Her hand went to her lips. She could still feel the intruder's fingers pressing into her face. Still smell his rancid breath. Still remember the fear that had seized her.

His threat repeated in her head.

You don't know what you've done.

What did that even mean? Did she want to know?

She pressed her eyes shut a moment.

Not really.

Instead, she watched as Gabe turned toward her,

his hand on his side—the side she'd stitched up earlier today.

Had he been hurt again?

Uneasiness rippled through her. That was the last thing she wanted.

She rushed down the steps to meet him. "Are you okay? What happened?"

He nodded, but Autumn couldn't ignore the frustration in his eyes. He'd wanted to catch that guy. If he hadn't been injured earlier, he probably would have.

"I'm fine. I'm more concerned about you. Did he hurt you?"

"No, he just scared me mostly. At least that's all he had time to do. If you hadn't shown up when you did . . ." She shivered.

Autumn couldn't finish her sentence. She was fairly certain the man hadn't intended to kill her, but he'd definitely wanted to make it clear that he would if it came down to it.

Gabe straightened, still studying her with concern. "Did you call the police?"

"I did. They're on their way."

"We need to get you back into the house. I don't like you being out here. You're too exposed." His gaze scanned the area around them, clearly still on the lookout for trouble.

"Of course." Her gaze went to his side again. He kept touching it like something bothered him.

She'd given him strict instructions to stay off of his feet. He clearly hadn't listened. Yet how could she scold him after what he'd done.

Autumn led him back inside and locked the door behind her. Once they were in the living room, she turned to Gabe. "I need to see your stitches."

"I'm fine." He waved a hand in the air.

"If you're fine, then let me see your stitches."

He hesitated another moment before begrudgingly pulling up the hem of his shirt.

Autumn shook her head at what she saw. Two stitches had pulled loose.

"I'm going to need to fix those," she murmured.

Gabe's eyes closed slightly. "I'm sure they'll be fine. Just put a butterfly bandage on it."

She gave him a pointed look. "I'm going to fix them either here or at the clinic. Take your pick."

After another moment of hesitation, Gabe finally nodded. "Fine. Clearly, arguing will do no good."

But before she could grab her supplies, the police arrived. Autumn gave them a statement, and they checked the place for evidence. Two other officers were on the lookout for any suspicious vehicles, but Autumn didn't have high hopes it would be found.

When they left, Autumn disappeared into the back and grabbed the supplies she needed. She always kept some medical necessities on hand, just in case.

She pointed to the couch. "Sit."

Gabe's eyebrows shot up. "Yes, ma'am."

After he lowered himself onto the cushions, she sat behind him, frowning as she studied his cut. "We've got to keep this wound clean."

"That's my goal."

"I'm sure it is," she murmured.

Autumn leaned closer to clean it, and she caught a whiff of his spicy aftershave. Earlier, he'd been covered in ditch water. But right now, he smelled clean and pleasant.

Why was she noticing this? She stitched up patients all the time, and she'd never paid attention to smells before. Not like this, at least.

As she cleaned the area around Gabe's wound, she frowned. "I've had to treat you twice in one day. I can already tell you're not going to be a very good patient. You're clearly not good at following doctor's orders."

He let out a quick chuckle. "Strangely enough, I've heard that before."

"I'm sure you have." Gabe seemed like the rambunctious type who might not look before leaping. Then again, he'd been a SEAL. Autumn was pretty sure acting on impulse wouldn't fly in his former line of work.

"Do you want me to numb you?"

"Not really. That hurts worse than the actual stitches."

"Very well." But as soon as Autumn pierced Gabe's skin, he winced. She needed to get him talking about something else to distract him.

But he beat her to the punch.

"Can you tell me what happened?" he started. "I know you told the police, and I overheard part of that. But I want to hear it again, if you don't mind."

Autumn let out a sigh, wishing she could just forget about it. But she couldn't. Not if she wanted to help catch this intruder.

"I came home from work and went into my bedroom. I noticed the light wasn't working in that one room, so I just assumed the bulb had blown out. I went to grab some clothes, and I heard a sound behind me. That's when the man grabbed me."

Gabe tensed beneath her hands. "Did he say anything?"

"He said, 'You have no idea what you've done.'"

"What?" Gabe's muscles bristled. "I don't like the sound of that."

"Believe me, neither do I." Those words would no doubt haunt her for a long time.

Gabe glanced up at her, his gaze probing hers. "You have no idea why somebody would do this?"

Autumn licked her lips. There were only two people she could see being responsible for this. Had either of them followed her here? Was one of them trying to exact some type of revenge on her?

Either way, she didn't want to bring them up. She wanted to bury that old part of her life.

Autumn shook her head, trying to hide the memories, the suspicions. "No, not really."

After she finished suturing the wound, she leaned back. "All done."

Gabe dropped his shirt back into place and turned toward her. "Thank you."

"No. Thank you." She paused and observed him for a moment. "By the way, what brought you past here tonight?"

A strange look swept through his gaze. "I just happened to be in the area and heard you scream."

She blinked at his simple explanation. "Talk about good timing."

"Absolutely." He stood and cleared his throat. "How about if I check out that bedroom light for you and make sure your doors and windows are secure?"

Autumn nodded. She'd been independent for a long time, but it was nice to have someone double-check things behind her.

"That sounds great. Thank you."

"It's the least I can do."

CHAPTER FIVE

THE LIGHT BULB hadn't been burnt out.

Someone had gone through some trouble to make sure they caught Autumn off guard.

Gabe found the breaker he was looking for and flipped it back on. Someone had clearly done this on purpose . . . that wasn't even a question.

Why? What about the doctor had precipitated this event? He didn't know, but he didn't like it.

He finished checking the doors and windows and felt confident the place was secure. But still he lingered.

Part of him didn't want to leave. Part of him was afraid trouble would return. Yet he didn't know Dr. Spenser well enough to insist on staying on her couch.

"I'll be fine." Autumn seemed to read his mind.

Gabe forced himself not to stare at her. Even in her disheveled state, she still looked beautiful. But that was beside the point right now.

He cleared his throat. "I'm going to give you my number. If you need anything at all or if you hear any strange noises, I want you to give me a call."

"Of course."

She grabbed a pad and pen from the kitchen counter and handed them to him. He wrote down his number before stepping back.

"Thank you again," she said. "Sounds like God was really watching out for me tonight when He sent you this way."

Guilt flooded him. Gabe really should admit that he'd stopped by to give her a shirt. He'd dropped it, hadn't he? He made a mental note to grab it on his way out. He didn't think the police had grabbed it.

But something stopped him from filling in the details for Autumn. A surge of self-consciousness, he supposed. Stopping by unannounced with something so trivial seemed inconsequential after what had happened.

"I'm glad I was here when I was." He started toward the door and offered another nod. All the suave things he'd thought to say tonight disappeared from his mind. That had a tendency to happen when he was around the doctor. "I guess I'll see you later."

"I'd like for you to stop by the clinic tomorrow, please. I want to check out the stitches one more time."

Another excuse to be around her? That sounded good to him. "I'll see you then."

She flashed a small smile. "Have a good night, Gabe."

He liked it when she said his name. He liked it a little too much.

He looked back one more time before reaching for the door handle. "Call me if you need me."

She offered a gentle smile. "I will."

AUTUMN SHIVERED as she glanced around. She knew Gabe had checked things out, but she still felt uneasy.

Why had that man been at her house? How had he gotten inside? What exactly would he have done if Gabe hadn't shown up when he did?

She shivered again.

If there was one thing she'd never enjoyed doing, it was living alone. Growing up, her house had been full. She had five brothers and sisters. Even when she'd gone away to college and then medical school, she'd always had roommates.

But she didn't have any here. She told herself it was better that way. That privacy would be her friend.

As another shiver traveled down her spine, she walked to the kitchen cabinet. She reached beneath the sink and pulled out a small, portable safe. Using her fingerprint, she unlocked it and picked up the gun nestled inside.

She stared at the Glock. She'd taken shooting lessons back in Maryland. Gotten her concealed carry permit. Had tried to stay up to date on how to use it by going to the shooting range as frequently as she could.

She prayed the day never came when she would have to pull the trigger on someone.

But she wanted to have it just in case.

When she'd told Stanley that she was taking shooting lessons, he'd scoffed at her. Judged her. Told her it was her job to save lives—not to play God.

Looking back now, it seemed ironic that those words had come from his lips.

She frowned at the thought of him. If only she could go back and redo that time in her life. But she couldn't. All she could do now was learn lessons from the mistakes she'd made.

And Stanley had been one of the biggest. It was a truly humbling time in her life when she realized that she wasn't as smart as she thought she was. In fact, the wool had been pulled right over her eyes.

As she held her gun, her thoughts drifted to Gabe. He was nothing like Stanley. Stanley pretended like he was strong when he wasn't. He didn't even know how to hang a mirror on her bathroom wall. For all of his cockiness, he was just a poser, someone who knew how to smile and get what he wanted. Someone who knew how to look good when needed.

He wasn't all bad. But he'd hurt Autumn enough that she would never think highly of him.

Gabe, on the other hand, had proven himself capable. Even though they were around the same age, there was something boyish about him. In some ways, he seemed years ahead of her. In other ways, he reminded her of a teenager.

The combination made her head spin . . . but something about it also intrigued her.

She looked at the gun again, double-checking that it was loaded and that the safety was on.

She would sleep with it beside her bed tonight.

That was, if she managed to get any sleep.

CHAPTER SIX

GABE SAT at his morning briefing with the rest of his team while assignments were distributed.

As Colton handed him his dossier, he opened the folder and frowned. This assignment would take him to Florida.

Florida? That was the last place he wanted to be. Not only was it miserably hot in August, but it was too far away from the trouble here—trouble he'd already invested himself in.

"Do you have a problem, Gabe?" Colton asked.

Gabe looked up and saw Colton studying him.

He shrugged. His military training had taught him to never argue with a superior. But there was nothing wrong with a good discussion, right?

"Respectfully, sir, I'd like to stay here on Lantern

Beach."

Colton cocked an eyebrow. "Why is that?"

Gabe figured he should start with the obvious. "I'm still recovering from the accident yesterday."

"That seems a valid concern. But this assignment doesn't start for three more days so I figured that you might be okay."

"And there's also the matter of Autumn."

"Autumn?" Amusement tinged Colton's voice.

"Dr. Spenser." Gabe quickly corrected himself.

That was right. Dr. Autumn Spenser. The woman who was totally out of his league. Someone like her wouldn't give Gabe a second look. But that didn't mean he wasn't going to try.

"After what happened last night, I'm concerned about her," Gabe finally said.

"She hasn't requested our help," Colton reminded him.

"I'm aware of that, and I don't want to overstep. But somebody broke into her place last night for a purpose. I don't like where I think this is going."

"I understand your concern, but we have to be careful about inserting ourselves in situations where we're not invited."

Disappointment filled him. But his leader was right. There were boundaries in place. "I understand. It's just that I don't think Autumn is the type who'd actually ask for help."

Colton stared at him a moment before nodding. "We still have three days until you're supposed to leave. Let's see what happens. See how you recover. We'll reevaluate in a couple of days. In the meantime, you can be close by in case something else comes up with Autumn."

"Thank you, sir."

Colton lifted a stack of folders. "Our jobs have been coming in quickly, which is a good and bad thing."

"There are only eight of us, and you usually head up things here," Rocco said. "So, what does this mean for us? The last thing we want is to be stretched too thin. It will affect the quality of our work."

"I agree. Ty and I have been meeting, and we are looking to hire some new recruits. We've grown much faster than any of us anticipated. Clearly, people who do what we do are in high demand. I just wanted to keep you informed and let you know that we're looking at hiring more people."

Gabe thought that sounded like a great idea. Last week, he'd heard Colton say they'd had to turn down some jobs because they were understaffed.

As the meeting wrapped up, he glanced at his watch.

Ordinarily, he would have already worked out by now. But he couldn't. Not with his current injuries. He felt even worse today than he had yesterday, just as he'd suspected. His whole body ached from the impact of that car hitting him.

Which reminded him, he'd promised Dr. Spenser he'd go in for another checkup.

Not that he would have forgotten. He wanted to see her again. Make sure she was still doing okay.

Because last night's incident wouldn't leave his mind.

DURING A BREAK BETWEEN PATIENTS, Autumn headed toward her office. She wanted to follow up on that call she'd made to Dr. Johnson yesterday. She was surprised she hadn't heard back from him yet, at least a confirmation that he'd gotten her message.

"Dr. Spenser, how are things going?" Doc Clemson stopped her before she reached her door.

Doc Clemson had been a doctor on the island for decades. He'd recently hired Autumn so he could cut back his hours. He also served as the Lantern Beach medical examiner.

The man had ruddy skin, thinning orangish-yellow hair, and a gregarious smile.

He was quite the figure on the island. Everyone loved him and his sidekick, former police chief and current mayor Mac MacArthur.

She remembered last night's events but decided not to mention them to Doc Clemson. What she really wanted was to stay under the radar. "I'm doing just fine."

"I'm so glad to hear that." The doc crossed his arms, seeming in no hurry to leave. "I see you're becoming acquainted with Blackout."

She raised her eyebrows. "You heard that, did you?"

"Word travels quickly on such a small island." He flashed a grin. "If they're not paying us visits, then they're not doing their jobs. There's a certain level of danger that comes with their skill set."

"I've noticed." Gabe and his team . . . their job was so different than hers but important, none-theless.

Clemson stepped away and paused. "Ernestine and I would like to have you over to eat with us when we're able to schedule a good time."

"That would be nice. I'd like that." Ernestine was Doc Clemson's longtime girlfriend and the island's former newspaper editor. From what Autumn knew about her, the woman was a bit of a recluse. But she seemed to make the doc happy.

"When you do come, you're welcome to bring somebody with you." He wiggled his eyebrows.

It seemed like everyone on this island wanted to play matchmaker for her. A couple of nurses had wanted to introduce Autumn to various single men they knew.

Autumn shook her head. "If that's a prerequisite then I won't be able to make it I'm afraid."

He offered a smile. "I understand. You're invited with or without a plus one, but I'll make my special blackberry pie if you bring someone with you."

"Good to know—but don't hold your breath."

"Not even for my pie?" His tone remained teasing and light.

She laughed. "It's tempting, but no."

They said goodbye, and she slipped into her office. She closed the door behind her and then pulled out her phone.

She dialed Dr. Johnson's number and listened as it rang.

But her mentor still didn't answer.

How strange. He'd always been so readily available in the past. Maybe he was on vacation or had lost his phone. Maybe he was teaching or in a meeting. There were numerous reasons why he might not pick up. Autumn would simply have to try again later.

In the meantime, she'd grab a quick snack. Working as a doctor, she had to eat whenever she could.

She opened her metal-sided lunchbox that she brought with her every day.

But as soon as she unlatched it and pulled the lid open, a chemical sprayed her in the face.

She jumped back and coughed, waving her hand in front of her.

What in the world was that?

Before she had time to contemplate what had happened or to get help, she felt her head spinning.

It must have been some type of gas. A sweet, antiseptic-like scent hung in the air. Chloroform?

She glanced at the door, wondering if she could make it to the hallway and find Doc Clemson or one of the nurses before the spray took full effect.

Instead, everything swirled around her before the darkness consumed her.

CHAPTER SEVEN

GABE STEPPED inside the clinic for his checkup and glanced around.

The women working behind the reception desk seemed preoccupied talking about the last medical drama on TV and hardly looked up. Instead of interrupting them, he slipped past and strode down the hallway toward Autumn's office.

He knew Autumn could be with a patient, but he knocked at her door anyway.

There was no answer.

Deciding to wait, he leaned against the wall.

As he inhaled the clean scent of the clinic, a slew of bad memories filled him—just as they did every time he came to a medical facility, which was more than his fair share.

His father had died in the hospital when Gabe was only eight. The last words he remembered his dad saying were, "You'll never amount to anything."

He'd blurted the words in a drunken rage—a rage fueled by the very alcohol that had ultimately caused his organs to shut down, leading to his death. Afterward, Gabe's mom had entertained a long line of boyfriends. Gabe had simply been another mouth to feed. A burden. A reason his mom's boyfriends hadn't wanted to stick around.

Gabe glanced at his watch. Fifteen minutes had already passed. Maybe he shouldn't have circumvented the reception area. For all he knew, Dr. Spenser could be handling an emergency right now.

However, he didn't think that was the case. Everybody around him seemed too relaxed to have any critical cases. There would be more urgency in the air.

Plus, there weren't that many rooms here at the clinic. If Gabe was right, he could see most of them from his position near Dr. Spenser's office.

Just then, Doc Clemson ambled down the hall and paused in front of him. "If it isn't Gabe Michaels. What brings you here?"

"I wanted to follow up with Dr. Spenser. I had a

little incident yesterday." He raised his shirt to show the doctor his scrapes, bruises, and stitches.

Doc Clemson made a face and shook his head. "That isn't good. You boys . . . you like to play rough, don't you?"

"There was no playing involved. Not on my end, not this time." Gabe shifted. "Do you know where Dr. Spenser is, by chance?"

He glanced at the door beside them. "Dr. Spenser was going into her office last I saw her. She's not with any patients. I just checked on them all myself."

A surge of alarm went through Gabe—perhaps a premature one, but he was on edge today. "She didn't answer when I knocked at her door."

A wrinkle formed on Doc Clemson's brow. "That's unlike her."

Clemson walked toward her office and pushed the door open. As Clemson called, "Hello?" Gabe heard the man's breath hitch.

Something was wrong.

He peered inside and spotted Autumn sprawled on the floor.

He sucked in a breath. What had happened?

Dear Lord . . . please help her be okay.

AUTUMN PULLED her eyes open and saw Doc Clemson and Gabe standing over her.

She blinked as memories slammed into her mind.

She remembered opening her lunch box.

Being sprayed.

Then . . . nothing.

She tried to sit up, but she felt so groggy. Instead, she rubbed her temples.

She must have hit her head when she passed out.

Doc Clemson shone a light into her eyes. "I don't think you have a concussion. What happened?"

As she pushed herself more upright, Clemson took one arm and Gabe the other.

Gabe? What was he doing here? Had he just happened to show up right when she needed him again?

Autumn wasn't sure what to think about that. But right now was no time to complain.

They helped her into her desk chair. Then Gabe stepped back and grabbed a cup of water from the dispenser behind him and handed it to her. "Maybe this will help."

She took a long sip, still trying to gather her bearings. How long had she been out?

"Did you have a medical episode?" Clemson lowered himself into the chair in front of her, his studious, fatherly gaze still on her.

She frowned as she shook her head. "No, not a medical episode. I opened my lunchbox and something sprayed me in the face."

Gabe stepped closer. "Something sprayed from your lunchbox?"

She nodded, even though the motion caused her head to throb. "I know it sounds crazy, but that's what happened."

She pointed to the container still on her desk.

Gabe reached for it before glancing at her. "Do you mind?"

"Not at all."

He took a surgical glove from a box on the filing cabinet behind him and slipped it on his hand. Then he nudged the lunchbox open and studied a canister that had been inserted there.

"It looks like someone superglued it in place," Gabe muttered. "Any idea what was inside this cylinder? As a medical professional, you probably have a better idea about it than I do."

Autumn rubbed her head. "My guess? Chloroform. It would've made me pass out."

Gabe frowned. "Is this why someone broke into your house last night?"

"Someone broke into your house last night?" Clemson looked at her, wrinkles of worry forming around his eyes.

Autumn resisted a scowl. She hadn't really wanted her boss to know about that. But there was no hiding it now. "That's right. Thank goodness Gabe got there when he did. The man ran off when he saw Gabe."

"Gabe went to your house last night too?" Surprise lilted Doc Clemson's voice.

Gabe shrugged. "The timing was uncanny."

She appreciated him not sharing any more details or feeding the rumor mill. Not that Doc Clemson was a gossip. But still.

"This couldn't have happened last night," Autumn said. "I packed my lunch this morning."

"Did you leave your lunchbox unattended today?" Gabe asked.

"It was in my office. I suppose someone could have slipped inside . . ."

"Why would somebody plant this in your lunchbox?" Doc Clemson sounded perplexed as he asked.

"That's a great question . . ." Autumn muttered as she rubbed her temples.

There was only one reason she could think of. But she really hadn't wanted to share it. However, it didn't look like she had much of a choice.

She let out a sigh before looking at Clemson and Gabe. "I'm not pointing fingers but . . ."

CHAPTER EIGHT

GABE SAT in the other chair next to Autumn's desk so he could listen to her explanation. He was curious about the worried look in her eyes—a look that appeared full of bad memories.

"There was a man named Byron Dimitri." Autumn's eyes contained a far-off expression, their depths mirrored with pain. "He was one of my patients back in Baltimore. He came in complaining of some lightheadedness and nausea. I ran some tests on him but couldn't find anything wrong. I actually did find evidence of heroin in his system, and I assumed his symptoms might be tied to that."

"What happened then?" Gabe asked.

"I recommended him to a specialist, but he never set up an appointment. A week later, he was rushed to the emergency room. Apparently, he had an aneurysm near his brain that wasn't detected in our tests. It hemorrhaged and . . ."

"I hate to hear that." Doc Clemson pressed his lips into a grim line. "But you did what you could."

Autumn let out a long breath and rubbed her hands together as if reliving the memories pained her.

"The family blamed me." Autumn's voice cracked. "Sued me. Raked my name through the mud. As far as they were concerned, Byron Dimitri's death was squarely my fault because of a failure to diagnosis his condition."

"And that led you to coming here?" Clemson asked as if this was all news to him.

She let out another long breath. "The other part of the story is that this guy's family had mob connections. They threatened me to the point where police had to send cars past my house to check on me."

"That's terrible," Clemson muttered.

"I got tired of living that way. Plus, for various reasons, I felt like it was time to move on. That's why I came here to Lantern Beach."

"So, you think somebody who's part of this family could have followed you here and made this threat against you?" Gabe asked.

Autumn shrugged, but each of her motions— even her expression—appeared heavy and burdened. "Like I said, I'm not pointing fingers. I just think it's a good possibility."

"Even if they're the ones responsible, why go through all this trouble?" Gabe's thoughts raced as he tried to put the pieces together.

Autumn rubbed her neck as if she didn't like that thought. "I have no idea. The only thing I can think of is that they want to ruin my life just like theirs was ruined when their brother died."

Gabe shifted, unsure how to bring up what he needed to say. Instead of thinking too hard, he dove in. "If you don't mind, I'd like to look into what's going on."

She glanced at him, an unreadable emotion in her gaze. Surprise? Caution? Intrigue? "That's nice of you, but . . ."

"But?" Gabe wasn't going to let her off the hook that easily. Autumn had no good reason to turn down his offer . . . did she?

"I'm afraid . . . I'm afraid personal protection isn't in my budget right now."

Gabe almost wanted to snort. That's what her hesitation had been about? "I'm not asking for money. I'm just asking that you let me help."

She still hesitated another moment before shrugging. "Let me think about it. Right now, I have some patients I need to see."

Doc Clemson stood. "You stay here and drink some water. I'll go do the rounds. Plus, you need to report this to the police. They need to know what's going on."

Autumn frowned but nodded. "Of course."

Doc Clemson turned to Gabe. "Gabe, I don't want to overstep, but I'd like for you to stay with her until the police get here. Are you okay with that, Dr. Spenser?"

She hesitated before agreeing. "Yes, that's fine."

Gabe guessed, based on the expression on Autumn's face, that she didn't like being told what to do. She was too smart to argue with her boss though.

But Gabe didn't mind keeping an eye on her. He'd feel better if he stayed close, whether Autumn wanted him to be there or not.

But he hoped she wouldn't mind his presence.

Maybe that was hoping too much, though.

———

AUTUMN FINISHED GIVING Officer Dillinger her statement. He then took her lunchbox into custody for testing. Maybe a print had been left or the police could trace the device that had released the chloroform, assuming that's what the substance was. The lab analysis would also confirm that, and Clemson had also ordered a toxicology test on her.

She hated for people to make a big fuss over her. But she knew there was no choice in this situation.

By the time Officer Dillinger left, Autumn felt as if she'd recovered from the spray of fumes in her face. But Gabe didn't look as convinced. He remained seated against the wall in the office, watching everything and being entirely quieter than she'd assumed he was capable of.

Finally, she stood and smoothed her white lab coat. "I appreciate you staying here with me, but it looks like you can go now."

She knew Gabe was concerned about her still. Probably concerned that somebody would come into the clinic and stage another threat of some sort. But she couldn't live the rest of her life with somebody always watching her back. It just wasn't practical.

Gabe stood and hesitated, almost as if refusing to step toward the door. "Have you made your decision yet?"

"I'm still thinking about it. But I'll let you know. I

appreciate your offer and everything that you've done to help so far."

Autumn meant the words. Gabe truly had been a lifesaver, and she really did appreciate everything he'd done.

But this was too much for her to take in right now. She needed to figure things out on her own.

Before she could step toward the door, her phone rang.

Dr. Johnson's name popped up on her screen.

She quickly excused herself and put the phone to her ear. But it wasn't Dr. Johnson's voice on the other end.

"Hi there," a woman said. "I just heard your message on my father's phone, and I wanted to give you a call back."

Autumn's lungs froze as she sensed bad news was coming.

"I'm sorry to tell you this, but my father passed away last night."

Autumn gasped and sank back into her chair. "What? I had no idea. I'm so sorry."

"We're all still reeling from our loss. I don't think any of us have fully comprehended it."

"If you don't mind me asking, what happened?"

"He was in a terrible auto accident. The police said he died on impact."

"An auto accident? I just can't believe this . . ." Autumn muttered, shaking her head. "Your father was a good man. He was doing important work."

"I know." A muffled cry sounded on the line. "We all know. Believe me."

But as Autumn thanked her and lowered the phone, a bad feeling swirled in her stomach.

Dead? How could Dr. Johnson possibly be dead?

CHAPTER NINE

GABE LISTENED to the conversation and sensed something was wrong. Autumn had lost someone, and her body language suddenly looked hunched with grief.

"I'm so sorry, Dr. Spenser," he murmured.

Autumn nodded, shock still capturing her features and a dazed look in her eyes. "Me too. I just can't believe this. Dr. Johnson was an outstanding man."

"Did the person who called say anything about his car accident?"

"His daughter only said that he died on impact." She narrowed her eyes. "Why are you asking?"

Gabe shrugged, trying not to add any more grief

to what Autumn already must be feeling. "Just wondering."

In his world, every death was viewed with suspicion. It was always the first place Gabe's mind went.

"Are you going to be okay?" He wished he could do more, that he could reach out to her. But it was too soon. He didn't know her that well.

Autumn nodded, but she didn't look as confident now as she had earlier. "I'll be fine. Thank you for asking."

He stepped back, unable to think of a good reason not to leave. "I can stay if you want."

She opened her mouth, almost as if about to accept his offer. Then she clamped her lips together and shook her head as if thinking better of it.

"Thank you, but I'll call you if I need anything."

Gabe nodded. He'd figured that was what she'd say. With resignation, he stepped toward the door.

"Oh, before you go, I need to see those stitches and make sure you're doing okay," Autumn called. "I'm assuming that's why you stopped by."

"Of course." Gabe paused before he reached the door.

Autumn seemed to set aside her grief for a moment as she rose and walked toward him.

Following her instructions, Gabe lifted his T-shirt so she could examine his wound.

As she touched the skin around his stitches, Gabe felt fire spread through his veins.

He swallowed hard, pushing the feeling down. This was just a routine medical check. There was nothing more to it, and Gabe shouldn't spin it otherwise.

"I did a pretty good job with this if I do say so myself." Autumn nodded as if proud of her work.

Gabe chuckled. "I'm glad. I'd hate to add any more scars to my already long list."

She straightened and looked him in the eye, curiosity glinting in her gaze. "How many do you have?"

"Fifteen and counting. I'm beating the rest of the guys."

"You've made this a contest?" She raised an eyebrow, not bothering to hide her disapproval.

"When it comes to my team, everything's a contest. It helps us get by. Well, that and sushi."

She raised her eyebrows even higher. "I can't say I've seen any sushi restaurants here on the island."

"There aren't any. But we're going to have to remedy that. Rocco was talking about possibly learning to make sushi himself. I think I'd rather go without it than trust his culinary skills though."

Autumn let out a chuckle, and her shoulders seemed to ease slightly. "You guys are certainly interesting."

Gabe stared at her another moment, at the beautiful waves of auburn hair that cascaded over her shoulders. At her intelligent green eyes. At the smattering of freckles across her cheeks and nose.

His opinion hadn't changed. Autumn Spenser was the most beautiful woman he'd ever laid eyes on.

"I guess I should go." He dragged the words out, still unable to think of a reasonable excuse to stay—without her permission, at least.

Autumn raised her gaze to meet his. As she did, her lips twitched and worry lined her gaze. "I'll call you."

"And if you run into any more trouble . . ."

"Then I'll *definitely* call you."

Gabe wished that made him feel better. But it didn't.

Because he knew that trouble could pop up before she had the chance to grab her phone.

AUTUMN TREATED a few more patients and worked on some paperwork. But her mind continued to wander back to Dr. Johnson.

She just couldn't believe her mentor was dead.

And why was Gabe asking questions about his accident? Did Gabe actually think the doctor's death wasn't truly an accident?

The thought was preposterous.

Except . . . what if it wasn't? After all, Dr. Johnson wasn't careless. He was the most detailed person Autumn had ever met. There was no way he would have been reckless on the road.

Maybe the weather had been bad the evening of his accident, It was the only explanation that made sense.

She frowned as she sat at her desk and thought everything through.

On impulse, she picked up her phone and called one of Dr. Johnson's colleagues, a man named Ken Walker. The two of them worked together at a research hospital outside of DC.

Dr. Walker answered on the first ring. "Autumn Spenser! It's always good to hear from you."

"I wish I was calling just to catch up. But, unfortunately, I'm calling because I heard about Dr. Johnson."

Ken's voice sobered. "We were all sorry to hear about his passing. I thought about calling you in case you hadn't heard. Then again, I just heard the news myself this morning, and I've been trying to process everything. I thought I'd wait until I heard about his funeral arrangements before making any calls."

"Can you give me any more details about what happened? I'm having a hard time comprehending this."

"From what I was told, Dr. Johnson was driving home from the hospital after a late-night shift when he veered off the road and hit a tree. The police assume he fell asleep at the wheel. He'd worked for nearly twenty-four hours straight."

"The police are assuming he fell asleep?" Alarm coursed through her. "There were no signs of foul play, right?"

"Not that I've heard about. Do you have reason to believe otherwise?"

"Oh no," Autumn rushed, not wanting to draw any attention to the issue until she'd thought it through more. "I guess I'm just still trying to sort through all of this information."

"I know. It's a lot."

Autumn picked up a pen and began scribbling

on the calendar in front of her—one of her nervous tics that she'd done even as a child. "How was Dr. Johnson acting before he died? I know it sounds like an odd question, but there's part of me that needs to know."

"He seemed mostly like himself."

"Mostly?" She hadn't missed how he'd thrown that word in. It wasn't insignificant.

Ken let out a long breath as if hesitating to share more. "The last time I met with Dr. Johnson was about a week ago. He said he was working on a new project."

Her pulse spiked at his revelation. "What kind of new project?"

"He didn't say. Dr. Johnson just indicated that a few things had popped up on his radar, and he was trying to put the pieces together."

Autumn leaned back and frowned, disappointed there wasn't any more news. "No other details?"

"No, I'm sorry. I don't know any other details. If you want to know more, you should talk to his research assistant, Sarah Andrews."

Autumn scribbled the woman's name on her paper. "Good to know. I'll keep her in mind."

As the call ended, Autumn sat quietly for several minutes. It would be time for her to leave soon. But the thought of walking alone into the parking lot to her car made her shiver.

Maybe she needed to rethink this bodyguard arrangement Gabe had offered. How exactly would that work? Especially with her being here at the clinic . . .

She didn't know, but it was definitely something that she could consider.

Because she had a feeling her troubles were far from over.

CHAPTER TEN

GABE DECIDED to go to one of his favorite restaurants, a place called The Crazy Chefette, after he left the clinic. Though the restaurant owner was known for her unique food creations, Gabe always ordered an ordinary ham and cheese omelet with home fries. He was a no-frills kind of guy.

His colleague Beckett Jones joined him there, which was good. Gabe needed someone to bounce his thoughts off of.

After they ordered their meals, Beckett started, "Hey, man. What's going on?"

As Gabe ran through the day's events, Beckett shook his head and clucked his tongue.

"That sounds like a crazy ride," Beckett said. "Any idea what's going on?"

Gabe told him about the Dimitri family.

Beckett rubbed a hand across his beard as his gaze drifted in thought. "Do you think one of these guys are here and trying to get revenge on Dr. Spenser?"

"I'm wondering if it's a possibility. It's a place to start, at least."

Gabe pulled out his phone and typed in Byron Dimitri's name. A few minutes later, pictures filled his screen. He frowned as he read more about Byron and his family.

"Apparently, two of his brothers have criminal records," he muttered. "One was even on a wanted list."

He showed the screen to Beckett so he could see the photos of Mario and Lucas Dimitri.

Beckett frowned as he scanned the various headlines about the men.

Before they could talk more, their food was delivered. They prayed silently before digging in.

"Text them to me, and I'll circulate these between the guys so they can keep their eyes open here on the island," Beckett said, not missing a beat. "We should send the information to Cassidy and her crew also. They need to know about this."

"I'll do that." Gabe planned on looking more into this himself too.

As he continued to study the photos another moment, he looked up, feeling Beckett's stare.

Gabe shifted, suddenly uncomfortable under his friend's scrutiny. "Everything okay?"

Amusement glimmered in Beckett's gaze. "I hate to be the one to say it, but you've got it bad . . ."

Gabe knew exactly what he was referring to: Autumn. But No-Smile Beckett had no room to talk. Gabe's colleague was suddenly grinning ear to ear now that he'd connected with Sami Reynolds.

"I'm not judging," Beckett continued. "I just know that from the moment you saw the pretty doctor, you couldn't take your eyes off of her."

"Your point?"

Beckett stared at him. "So, what are you going to do about it?"

That was an excellent question. Gabe frowned. "I'm still trying to figure that out."

Before they could talk more, a sound outside caught Gabe's ear.

A bang.

Followed by screams.

Gabe and Beckett jumped to their feet and rushed out to the parking lot.

AS AUTUMN WANDERED BACK toward her office, she couldn't deny the fact that she was on edge.

Every time someone new walked into the clinic, she tensed. She continually looked over her shoulder. Her muscles—especially around her neck—felt so tight that moving was uncomfortable.

Had Byron Dimitri's family found her here? And what were they trying to prove by breaking into her home? By making her pass out?

What would they do to her next time?

If she hadn't been discovered when she had, would someone have abducted her? Tried to kill her?

She shivered at the thought of it. She wasn't one to live in fear. But, right now, she was jumpier than grease in a hot frying pan.

"Are you still doing okay?"

She looked up from her electronic tablet as Doc Clemson paused in front of her. "I'm fine. Thank you."

"I can take over from here if you'd like." He nodded to the paperwork she was filling out.

She offered a grateful smile as she declined. "I

think I just have one more patient to see before my shift ends."

"Why don't you let me get them? It would be no problem."

She started to say no when she reconsidered. "Are you sure?"

"Of course. I wouldn't have offered otherwise."

After everything that had happened, she could use some time to sort her thoughts. "Thank you. I appreciate that."

But when she slipped into her office, she wasn't quite ready to leave. Was it because she dreaded leaving the safety of this building?

First, she wanted to call Dr. Johnson's research assistant, Sarah.

Autumn wasn't sure what she hoped to ascertain from the conversation. She knew there was a good chance that Dr. Johnson's death was just what it had been labeled: an accident. But she wouldn't rest until she knew more.

Especially since she now knew about the secret project he'd been working on.

Autumn had to go through several people before reaching Sarah. She finally came on the line, but Autumn got the sense she'd disturbed her.

"Am I catching you at a bad time?" Autumn asked.

"No, no. Not really. What do you need?" Her words came out fast and high-pitched.

"I'm curious if you knew what Dr. Johnson was working on." Autumn should have probably warmed up to the woman a little bit first, but the conversation hadn't lent itself to that.

Sarah hesitated a moment after Autumn asked the question. "Why do you want to know?"

"I'm just curious because I found out some information, and I wanted to get his input on it. Then I heard he had a secret project that left him acting out of sorts. It has me concerned, especially when I put the facts together."

"He didn't like to talk about it." Sarah's voice cracked.

Autumn's pulse quickened. "Why not?"

"Dr. Johnson said that until he had concrete proof, he couldn't share any information, that it wouldn't be wise."

"Now that he's passed away, who's going to pick up the torch for him on this project?"

"Funny that you mention that. He actually threw out your name. He thought you would be ideal to look over this information and he'd planned to get in touch with you. He just . . . never had the chance." A muffled cry sounded on the other end of the line.

Autumn's heart continued to thrum in her ears. "Is that right? I would have been honored. In fact, maybe I could still help by reviewing his work."

Sarah let out a long breath, hesitation marring the sound. "I don't know. I'm just not sure what I'm supposed to do."

"Seeing his project to completion would be the least I could do. Can you tell me what it was about? Give me some type of hint?"

Another moment of silence passed until finally Sarah said, "I'm not sure. I only know someone gave him a tip and asked him to look into something."

Autumn leaned back in her chair, even more confused now than she was when all this started.

BECKETT AND GABE stood on the sidewalk outside of The Crazy Chefette staring in the direction of the gunfire.

The crowd had scattered. Some people had hidden behind cars. A few people craned their necks, trying to see what was happening.

"That was just Drew Crabtree," someone said.

Gabe looked over at the sixty-something man wearing a fishing hat and vest. "Who?"

"He's one of the locals. Apparently, he was aiming at the sky when he pulled the trigger. Probably trying to scare away the birds before they destroyed the crop of collard greens he's growing in his backyard."

Gabe let out a breath. "Are you sure that's all it was?"

"That's what I overheard Drew's cousin Buddy saying to his friend Milton. The sound came from the direction of Drew's house. The police just pulled up there now."

Gabe followed his gaze and saw blue lights flashing behind some trees.

At least this didn't seem to be related to everything else that had happened. But each event had left Gabe on edge.

Now that Gabe and Beckett knew everyone was okay, they wandered back inside to their table.

But when they reached the booth, Gabe stared at the food in front of him.

"What's wrong?" Beckett asked.

"Is it just me or does my food look funny?"

Beckett squinted down at their plates. "What are you getting at, Gabe?"

"Somebody did something to my food."

"Why would they do that?"

Gabe frowned. "That's a great question."

"Are you sure?" Beckett glanced at Gabe's plate again, studying the omelet more closely.

Gabe pointed at the top of his omelet. "There's a white substance coating my eggs. I'm sure it wasn't there before. I've eaten this meal uncountable times."

Beckett called one of the waitresses, Olivia Rollins, over to their table.

"Hey, Olivia. Did you see anyone near our food when we went outside?"

Olivia glanced at the plates and shrugged. "Honestly, it got crazy in here. People started running every which way. Some people even rushed into the kitchen. I wish I could tell you if somebody stopped near your booth, but that was the last thing on my mind."

Gabe frowned. He wasn't making this up. He felt confident about that.

Had somebody lured them out of the restaurant just so they could tamper with his food?

Gabe didn't know. It sounded extreme. But either way, he was going to collect samples of this food and see what he could find out.

CHAPTER ELEVEN

GABE DECIDED to go straight to the police station with his food. He didn't know how fresh it needed to be in order to find any possible substances on it, but he figured the sooner the better.

But when he got there, Cassidy was in her office talking with Drew Crabtree, the man who'd discharged his firearm near The Crazy Chefette. Gabe had never met the man before, but he'd heard rumors about his reckless redneck tendencies.

Gabe decided to wait a few minutes until Cassidy was done. As he did, he settled in one of the chairs in the lobby and pulled out his phone.

Out of curiosity, he continued researching the Dimitri family. Numerous articles about them appeared and made it clear they were trouble. Not that Gabe was surprised. Not at all.

Though the family was large, the major players appeared to be Mario and Lucas, the brothers who ran a pot business out of their basement. Gabe headed to social media to see what he could discover there.

To his surprise, both brothers had pages. The pictures they posted made them look like a normal if not gregarious family.

But he noticed that the oldest brother, Mario, hadn't posted in the past week.

Could that be because Mario was here in Lantern Beach?

Gabe knew he could head to the ferry terminal and request to see the security footage of everyone coming and going from the island. He could check with the rental management companies and see if anybody with that name had rented a house in the area. But those tasks were tedious, and he wasn't sure he was at that point where he could justify that yet.

Instead, he looked up Mario Dimitri's phone number and decided to give him a call. Gabe was going to have to wing this conversation.

Three rings in, a woman answered.

Gabe straightened. "I'm trying to reach Mario Dimitri."

"Who is this?" The woman's voice sounded tense with suspicion.

"I'm Dan with the Mercedes dealership, and I'm calling about a recall on his Maybach." Gabe had seen a picture of the man's vehicle in one of the online photos and hoped that this might be a safe bet.

"Well, I'm afraid he's out of town right now."

"Isn't he lucky? This is a great time to be traveling." Gabe tried to sound conversational. "Beautiful weather. Great time of year."

"I suppose."

"Unfortunately, the matter I'm calling about is a safety recall. Do you think I could reach him while he's away? I'd really like to get this repair scheduled."

"Mario left explicit instructions that he shouldn't be disturbed. I'll let him know that you called when he gets back."

Disappointment filled him. But it had been worth a shot. "I appreciate your time."

Just as Gabe ended the call, Drew Crabtree stepped out of Cassidy's office and strode outside.

Cassidy appeared in her doorway. She motioned for him to join her in her office.

As soon as Gabe stepped inside, he placed the bag with the omelet on her desk. "I think this is poisoned. Is there a way you could check it out?"

She raised an eyebrow. "Poisoned?"

"I know it might sound crazy, but there's a white substance on the edges of the omelet. It wasn't there before I stepped outside to check on that gunfire."

"Better safe than sorry." Cassidy picked up the bag and examined it herself. "I'll see what I can do."

"I appreciate it." Gabe shifted in front of her, his thoughts turning back to yesterday's collision. "Any updates on that hit-and-run, by chance?"

She frowned. "We've been looking for the car and driver responsible, but we haven't had any leads. We've talked to people in the area, but no one saw a thing."

He wasn't surprised. But he was disappointed.

"We're still investigating this," she explained. "I want you to know that. Cases like this are hard because so little evidence is left behind."

Gabe understood, but he just needed a little ray of sunshine concerning this case. "If you hear something, will you let me know?"

"Of course." Cassidy lifted a folder on her desk. "How is Dr. Spenser doing today?"

The doctor's image flashed through Gabe's mind, and he fought a smile. "She seems to be okay, but I can only imagine how shaken she is after everything that happened."

"We sent some fingerprints off to be examined, but I don't have high hopes that we'll get any hits. We're doing everything we can to figure this out."

Before Gabe could respond, his phone buzzed. He looked down and a small grin curled his lips.

"Speaking of Autumn," he held up his phone, "she's calling now. Excuse me."

"I'll let you know as soon as we have any news."

AUTUMN'S THROAT clenched as she waited for Gabe to answer.

She'd holed herself up in her office and tried to convince herself she shouldn't call him. But talking to him was the most logical thing to do right now. If anyone had answers or if anybody could help her find answers, it was Gabe Michaels.

He answered a moment later, his voice sounding curious but casual. "Hey, Dr. Spenser."

"Please, just call me Autumn." He had been, but they might as well get that formality out of the way. "I was hoping you would answer."

"What's going on? Did something else happen?" Concern ricocheted through his voice.

She rubbed her throat, the tight muscles there making it hard to breathe. "No, nothing else has happened. Not really. But I was hoping we could talk."

"Of course. What exactly do you want to talk about?"

She pressed her lips together, hesitating before sharing her reasoning. This was something much more than a quick phone conversation could cover.

"I want to talk to you about the substance that was sprayed on you and your teammates when you were overseas."

Silence stretched across the line.

Finally, Gabe said, "Do you think this is relevant to something going on now?"

"It's a long story, and I'd love to speak with you. Face-to-face, preferably."

"We can do that. But I don't really feel comfortable with you being out in public right now. Not with everything that's happened."

She knew what he was getting at. She was a

target. The thought caused a flash of nausea to rise in her. How had her life turned into this?

"What do you suggest?" Her voice sounded scratchy as she asked the question.

"Let me pick you up, and I'll take you back to the Blackout headquarters. We can get something to eat in the cafeteria and talk. It will be safer there than it will be anywhere else."

Autumn had been curious about the Blackout facility located on the northern end of the island. Seeing it for herself and talking to Gabe somewhere safe seemed like a win-win. "Okay. Let's do that."

"Can I pick you up in thirty minutes? Or is that too soon?"

She glanced at her watch. "Thirty minutes would be perfect. I'm at the clinic."

"I'll see you then."

As Autumn ended the call, she realized that she was looking forward to seeing him entirely more than she should be.

CHAPTER TWELVE

GABE MADE a couple more calls to ensure that dinner would work. He didn't want anything fancy, and he wasn't trying to awkwardly read any more into the situation than he should. But he *would* like some privacy, and it would be nice if the meal was tasty.

He felt a rush of both excitement and nerves as he headed down the road to the clinic. If he'd known Autumn would be riding in his car, he would have cleaned it more.

Instead, he'd quickly collected a couple of old water bottles, three straw wrappers, and an old plastic bag and had stuffed them into his trunk before he had taken off down the road. He'd also put down the windows to help air it out a little bit. He'd left a wet bathing suit in here last week, and the musty stench wasn't quite gone yet.

His mom had always told him that his messiness would be the death of him one day. He hoped his mother wouldn't be right about this.

Gabe pulled up in front of the clinic and started to get out to find Autumn when she emerged through the door.

His throat went dry when he saw her. The woman really was gorgeous. If Gabe could spell out his dream woman, she would look exactly like Autumn.

Beautiful. Smart. Friendly.

Just as quickly, he averted his gaze. This was no time to be distracted. Not when Autumn's life could be on the line.

Instead, he scanned everything around them, searching for any signs of danger.

Nothing out of the ordinary caught his eye. Still, he refused to let his guard down.

He reached across the vehicle and opened the door, realizing he didn't have time to get out and properly open it for her. Autumn had gotten here too fast.

As she climbed inside, the pleasant scent of her perfume filled the space. It was much better than the aromas he'd smelled in his car earlier. Gabe wasn't much on identifying scents, but whatever Autumn wore reminded him of a meadow of wildflowers.

A meadow of wildflowers? Really, Gabe?

As soon as Autumn put her seatbelt on, Gabe took off down the road. It was only a ten-minute drive to Blackout. But he'd keep his eyes open for anything suspicious around them until he pulled through the gates at the campus.

"Thank you for doing this." Autumn's voice sounded scratchy, no doubt from the stress of everything that had happened.

"It's no problem," he said. "How did the rest of your day go?"

She shrugged, but something lingered beneath her gaze. "Workwise? It was fine. But I need to talk to you about a couple of things that have left me feeling uneasy."

Gabe's curiosity continued to grow. Just what had she discovered?

In the meantime, he told her about the gunfire near the restaurant earlier—including his suspicion about the food.

"You think someone tried to poison you?" Her lips parted in shock.

"I know it sounds crazy, but, yes, I do think that."

"Why does someone want you dead so badly?"

Her question hung in the air a moment until finally Gabe shrugged. "I wish I knew."

A few minutes later, they pulled through the gate at the Blackout campus, and Gabe parked in front of the Daniel Oliver Building.

"Here we are." He ran around to help her out and watched as she stood, taking it all in.

Together, they walked toward the front door.

He couldn't stop thinking about where this conversation would go.

Whatever Autumn had to say, Gabe knew it was a big deal.

He prayed he'd have the right words to say and the proper advice to give, especially when he remembered how high the stakes were.

AUTUMN PAUSED and glanced at the massive three-story building in front of her. It almost looked like a beachside hotel with two wings stretching from the center doors. Dormers had been built onto the roof, gray siding covered the walls, and a large porch welcomed people as they arrived.

"This place is bigger than I thought it would be."

She stared at the name written above the door, barely visibly in the fading sunlight. "Why is it named Daniel Oliver Building?"

Gabe's lips twitched as if he fought a frown. "Daniel was a former SEAL. He gave his life to keep thousands of people safe. Naming the building after him was the least we could do."

Autumn glanced at him, something welling deep inside her. Admiration? Maybe.

What these guys did was sacrificial. Brave. Amazing. They put their lives on the line to save others, to protect freedoms, to avert crises. They may not have endured years of medical school, but they'd endured years of training—some on the field and some in the direct line of danger.

Who wouldn't admire that?

She pressed her lips together, suddenly feeling out of place on the campus of these people she admired so much. "Are you sure it's okay that I'm here?"

"I ran it past my boss first. He's fine with it."

"I find what you're doing fascinating, and I'm excited to be here."

"Are you?" Light filled Gabe's gaze.

Light . . . and something else.

Was that a spark of attraction?

Part of her was flattered.

Not that Autumn wanted to date right now. Not after what happened with Stanley. Had her heart fully recovered? Would it ever?

Even as she wanted to deny that she was attracted to Gabe, as soon as he placed his hand on the small of her back to guide her inside, a ripple rushed through her.

What was that about? Letting her feelings get the best of her was so unlike her.

Before she could overthink it, Gabe led her up the steps and in through the front door, whisking her away from the analytical thoughts she was tempted to indulge in.

"After we eat, I can give you a quick tour," Gabe said. "But we're right on time to pick up our food."

"That sounds great."

They swung by the cafeteria, and Gabe grabbed a bag full of food. Then he led her to a small table outside, away from everybody else but nestled behind three walls. It faced the Pamlico Sound in the distance, and the little nook felt safe and cozy.

Safety was a feeling Autumn welcomed, especially after everything that had happened.

He pulled out some food containers. "I didn't

know what you liked, so I took the liberty of ordering my two favorites."

"What have you got?" Autumn really wasn't that picky, but she appreciated Gabe's thoughtfulness.

"I have stuffed shells with our chef's famous marinara or tilapia with a cream sauce and rice."

"Hmm . . . I think I'll take the stuffed shells—unless that's what you want."

"I'm good with either." He set the containers in front of them as well as some silverware and bottled water. "Sorry this isn't anything nicer."

"I'm just grateful you're meeting with me." As the reality of their upcoming conversation settled on her, Autumn instantly sobered.

She wasn't sure how he was going to respond to the questions she needed to ask, nor was she sure how he might receive her theories. But she had no choice but to move forward. They'd come this far, and there was no turning back now.

She prayed that she had the right words . . . because what she had to say could possibly open up old wounds, and her doctor's orders for him had been to rest and heal.

CHAPTER THIRTEEN

"WOULD you mind telling me about the mission you mentioned to me?" Autumn picked at her food as she turned toward Gabe. "The one where you said a chemical was sprayed on you?"

Gabe put his fork on the table, suddenly not that hungry.

He had no idea where Autumn was going with this, especially in light of everything that happened. Didn't they have bigger worries right now?

He'd been injured in a hit-and-run. Somebody had broken into Autumn's house and then rigged a canister to spray a substance into her face.

So why was she bringing up one of Gabe's past missions?

He didn't ask. Not yet. Because he figured that

Autumn had a good reason for this conversation. He just needed to be patient.

He swallowed hard before starting. "It happened during a job in Africa. It was called Operation Grandiose. That mission changed all of us—and probably not for the better."

Autumn put her own fork down and turned her full attention on him, her demeanor professional but curious and compassionate. "Do you mind talking about it?"

That was a good question. Did he mind? The operation wasn't something he usually brought up. None of his team did. Not really, at least. Not the details.

They kept the experience locked away so they didn't have to relive any of those horrible moments.

He was a former SEAL. He'd trained to be the toughest of the toughest. Certainly, that meant he could handle a conversation like this.

He sucked in another breath. "What do you want to know?"

"Anything that you'd be willing to share."

His mind drifted back in time to the last big mission his team had done when they'd been SEALs.

"There were eight of us on the mission all together," he started. "Me, Beckett, Rocco, and Axel, along with four guys from other teams. We were sent outside of Nairobi to the jungle. I'd never experienced anything like what we encountered there."

"I can only imagine."

"Everything about our operation was high risk—our targets, the landscape, the snakes."

"Snakes?" She raised her eyebrows, her body language making it clear she was listening to every word, watching his every movement.

Gabe nodded as he remembered his first encounter with a black mamba. He was still on the fence about what was scarier: the snake or terrorists.

"I didn't mind snakes until that trip when I came face-to-face with a black mamba—a snake with venom that can kill a person in twenty minutes," he told her. "But that's a story for another day. Anyway, the team parachuted in, and we knew that once we were on the ground that we were on our own. If we needed help, we were out of luck."

"That sounds terrifying."

"We'd done missions like that before, but never one with stakes that high."

Her gaze narrowed. "What was your objective?"

"The leader of a terrorist group, a man named Barmasai was supposedly hiding out at that location.

We only had a very narrow window of time to go in and take him out. This guy . . . he was bad news. He'd kidnapped the girls from a local boarding school and took them to his headquarters so he could profit off them. That was one of many illegal activities he'd been involved with."

Autumn rubbed her arm as if suddenly chilled. "I'm surprised I didn't hear about this on the news."

"The military kept it under wraps. For various reasons. But, really, as many operations that we can keep quiet, the better it is. Almost no one on the team wants the attention. We don't want people to think we're action stars. We just want to do the job and do it well."

"That's admirable."

"Anyway . . ." Gabe rubbed his neck as memories pummeled him.

If he closed his eyes, he was certain the scent of the jungle would return to him. The smell of sweat. Of gunpowder.

Of fear.

He swallowed hard. "We managed to find the location. The compound was heavily armed with guards, but we got through them and into the facilities. Inside, it was dark and the hallways were like a maze. Not only that, but booby traps had been set."

"Is that when they sprayed that gas on you?"

Gabe nodded and let out a long breath. The scent—sickly sweet—filled his mind. As a SEAL, he rarely panicked.

But he'd felt panicked at that moment.

Things like that were hard to forget, no matter how much he might want to.

"We all thought we were going to die right then and there, but we didn't," he continued. "However, once we were inside this compound where Barmasai was hiding out, we were ambushed. We were trapped there for six days straight, fighting for our lives with no sleep. To say it was horrible would be an understatement."

Autumn frowned. "I'm really sorry to hear about that. Truly."

Gabe locked gazes with her. "Now, do you mind telling me why you're asking about this?"

AUTUMN LICKED HER LIPS, still unsure how the conversation would go from here. But Gabe deserved the truth. She just hoped she delivered it with the empathy Gabe deserved.

She shifted in the patio chair and sucked in a

long, deep breath before starting. "I called some people to follow up about my mentor's death."

"Dr. Johnson?"

She nodded, still unable to believe he was dead. "Yes. It turns out that he was working on a top-secret project."

Gabe straightened but his gaze remained on her. "Is that right?"

"I'm still not 100 percent sure what his subject matter was, but he wanted to consult with me to get my opinions on his findings."

"Do you think whatever he was researching ultimately got him killed?"

That was the theory that kept replaying in her mind. Was she crazy? Reading too much into this?

She was about to find out.

"I'm trying not to jump to any conclusions." Autumn rubbed her neck, feeling the tension pulling there. "I clearly don't know what's happening here. All I know is that my instincts are telling me that something isn't right about what happened to you."

Gabe narrowed his eyes as he studied her face. "Is there a reason why Dr. Johnson might have wanted to consult with you?"

She picked up her fork again and stabbed at her

food, even though she was no longer hungry. "While I was in med school, my specialty was blood pathogens. He was my mentor, and we were both very passionate about the subject."

Gabe twisted his head, questions haunting his gaze. "I'm still not sure what this has to do with me."

She set her fork down, her distraction short-lived. She couldn't remember the last time she'd felt this nervous. "You have to remember that the original reason I contacted Dr. Johnson was because of what you told me when you came in after the hit-and-run. I thought about the different ailments you and your friends were experiencing, and I sent a sample of your blood to Dr. Johnson so he could examine it."

"I suppose that's all null and void right now."

"Yes, but he died after I sent it. The timing makes me wonder if there was any connection."

"To my hit-and-run and the death of your doctor friend?" Gabe's voice sounded strained, almost as if he'd begun picking up on the bigger picture.

Autumn shrugged and leaned closer, knowing this was a make-or-break moment in their conversation. "I know how it sounds. Crazy. But I want to know what they sprayed on you and why it's all affecting each of you in different ways."

Gabe's expression remained neutral. "I appreciate your concern, but we were all checked out."

"By whom?"

"Military doctors."

Her gaze narrowed. An objective physician would have been preferable or someone who specialized in chemical pathogens.

Gabe tilted his head. "What's that look for? You don't think military doctors can be trusted?"

"No, it's not that. There's just something about the situation that makes me feel unsettled. I keep thinking that you guys have been an advocate for so many people. You've saved so many lives. But who advocates for you?"

He stared at her a moment, an unreadable expression in his eyes.

She'd offended him, hadn't she? She'd taken this too far.

She should have never inserted herself in this situation.

She stood and grabbed her purse. "I'm sorry, Gabe. I should have minded my own business . . ."

Gabe rushed to his feet. "Autumn, it's okay. It's just that . . . I don't hear things like that very often."

Her shoulders relaxed slightly. That hadn't been the reaction she'd expected. "Things like what?"

"It's not often that people want to advocate for me." His voice sounded husky with emotion. "You're right. Sometimes it feels like my team was sent out on unthinkable missions. Then we had to come back and try to pretend like what we'd been through hadn't happened."

She stared at Gabe a moment, trying to fully grasp how he must feel. Either way, what his team had gone through wasn't fair. It wasn't right.

And she wanted to do something about it.

Autumn licked her lips before asking, "Do you mind if I keep looking into it?"

"Keep following your gut. Absolutely."

They stared at each other another moment before they both lowered themselves back into their seats.

Autumn released the breath she'd been holding in. She was glad to have that over with. But the strain of this situation was far from over.

Gabe turned to her, his gaze still appearing unsettled. "There's something I actually want to tell you also, Autumn. I've been doing my own research, and it turns out that Mario Dimitri hasn't been seen in a week. He's out of town, but his wife won't tell me where."

Autumn felt the blood drain from her face as she

realized the implications of his statement. "Do you think he's in Lantern Beach?"

Gabe shrugged. "I'm not sure. But after everything that happened to you, that would make the most sense."

CHAPTER FOURTEEN

GABE COULDN'T STOP REELING from the conversation.

He hadn't expected their talk to go so deep so fast. He hadn't expected it to feel easy to talk to Autumn and to open up about what had happened —especially to talk about what had happened during one of the most painful times in his life.

Hearing her say that she wanted to advocate for him? The notion had done something strange to his heart.

Gabe thought Autumn was beautiful and smart. But hearing that she wanted to look out for him had taken everything to a different level.

He knew that he—and his heart—were in serious trouble.

"Listen, I'm not sure where this will get me, but my team . . . we have some contacts in law enforcement. I could make a few calls about your friend's death and see if there's anything more to it than what the media has reported or told the family."

Autumn's eyes widened. "You would do that?"

"Of course. Like I said, I can't guarantee what I might learn. But I'm willing to give it a shot."

"Thank you. I really appreciate that."

As their gazes locked, he felt electricity spread through him.

He looked away before Autumn could sense his attraction.

This didn't seem like the time to bring that up.

Instead, he glanced at their food on the table. "I guess that's gotten cold."

Autumn offered a soft smile. "I guess it has. The few bites I took were really good."

He smiled at her attempt to be polite. "I have a better idea."

"What's that?"

"I happen to know that there's a hot fudge sundae bar in the cafeteria. What do you say we bypass dinner and go straight for dessert?"

A grin slowly spread across her face. "I think that sounds great."

Gabe collected their food, putting it into the bag, and then they both stepped back inside the Daniel Oliver Building.

"I just can't get over this place." Autumn continued to survey the massive three-story lobby with a fireplace as the centerpiece.

"It is pretty great, isn't it? Colton was just saying a few days ago that he never imagined when he and Ty Chambers started this organization that it would turn into what it has. But it's growing quickly. We're about to hire some more former military to work here."

"That's exciting that you get to be a part of something like this. I'm sure it brings you a lot of fulfillment."

"It really does. It's been a real lifesaver."

They stepped into the cafeteria and headed toward the table in the distance where dessert was set up. But before they reached it, Colton approached them. He quickly said hello to Autumn before pulling Gabe aside.

Gabe automatically knew something was wrong.

"I just got a call," Colton said. "Park rangers found Mikey's body. It looks like he fell off a cliff while hiking."

The air left Gabe's lungs. "What?"

Colton's jaw hardened. "I think we both know at this point that these deaths haven't been accidents. I just told the rest of the guys. We need to get to the bottom of whatever is going on."

Gabe ran a hand through his hair. "Yes, we do."

AUTUMN OVERHEARD PART of the conversation between Gabe and Colton. She didn't know what was going on, but it sounded dangerous.

Still, she didn't ask any questions. Not yet. Nor was she surprised when Gabe joined her and told her that dessert was going to have to wait.

His gaze probed hers, a new layer of intensity hovering there. "I hate to cut this short, but do you mind if I take you back to your car? Unfortunately, there are some things I need to do."

"Of course."

She didn't say much as they walked outside and climbed into his vehicle. But as they headed down the road, she couldn't stay quiet any longer.

"Do you want to talk about it?" she asked softly.

Gabe let out a breath, tension emanating from him. He didn't say anything for a moment, and Autumn was certain he wasn't going to answer.

But after several seconds of silence, he said, "Three Navy SEALs I've worked with have died recently."

"What?" She sucked in a breath at his words. Even though she'd known that happened—since she'd overheard part of the conversation—hearing the statement drove home the reality of the situation.

"We just got confirmation on the third one." He rubbed his jaw, which looked locked and tight.

"I'm so sorry, Gabe. If you don't mind me asking, how did they die?"

"The first in a car accident. The second in home invasion. The third fell off a cliff while hiking."

Autumn shook her head. All in different ways—none of which might seem like murder until you lined each death up, side by side. "So you think someone killed them and set it up to look like accidents?"

"It's the only thing that makes sense. They all happened in different areas of the country, so the police investigating each individual case aren't going to think much of what happened. But when you look at the complete picture, it's clear something is going on."

"Oh, Gabe . . . I'm so sorry. These are all guys from your SEAL team?"

He frowned, his facial muscles still taut, his gaze still intense. "They weren't all on my team. But we all worked Operation Grandiose together."

Her head pounded at each new reveal. Her analytical brain raced ahead, trying to put together the pieces, but to no avail. Did this somehow tie in with her research as well? Was that too much of a stretch?

Maybe.

But maybe not.

"Why would someone try to kill all of you?" she asked.

"I think it's clear that we're on some type of hit list. There could be any number of reasons why."

"But this one clearly goes back to that operation in Africa."

His jaw jumped as he stared at the road ahead. "Yes, it seems to."

"I'm sorry to hear about this, Gabe. Does this explain the hit-and-run you were involved in?"

"That's my best guess." As he said the words, he looked into the rearview mirror. "Speaking of which . . ."

Autumn saw his shoulders tighten and knew something was wrong. "Gabe?"

"I think we're being followed."

She glanced behind her as a shot of fear made her back go ramrod straight. "How do you know?"

"Instinct. Experience. The car behind us has been following us at the exact same distance. The driver turned behind us at the first street we passed coming from Blackout. No one hardly ever goes down that way."

Autumn gripped her armrest. She didn't like the sound of this. "What are you going to do?"

"Is your seatbelt on?"

Her stomach dropped at the implications of his statement. "Of course. Always."

"I've got to lose this guy. First, I need to figure out for sure that he's following us."

"Do what you have to do," she said. "But don't be surprised if I scream."

CHAPTER FIFTEEN

GABE ACCELERATED. He didn't want to go too much over the speed limit. Didn't want to put anybody else at risk so he could get away from this guy.

But he was afraid the driver following him would try to run them off the road or do something else foolish. He needed to make sure that didn't happen.

He felt apprehension rising in waves from Autumn beside him. He hated that she was in this position. Hated that she had to go through this with him.

But, right now, his only goal was to keep her safe.

And safety meant getting away from this guy.

Gabe glanced in the mirror again and saw the headlights getting closer. He also knew he was approaching a more congested area of town. Tourists could easily be crossing the street to get from the ice cream shop to a gift shop.

Nobody else needed to be hurt here. In fact, Gabe wouldn't forgive himself if that happened.

He kept his pace slow and his eyes open as he went through the retail tourist district. As soon as he reached the end of that, he pressed his accelerator again.

He headed toward the south end of the island where the lighthouse was located. It was remote out there, surrounded by the woods of a national forest and seashore.

Remoteness could be good and bad news.

As he saw the headlights getting closer again, he pushed the accelerator harder.

"Gabe?" Autumn's voice wavered beside him.

"I'm sorry, Autumn. I wish I could drop you off somewhere. I wish I felt confident that if I did that, you wouldn't be hurt. But that's not the case." Anger burned through his veins at the thought of Autumn being in danger—especially at the thought of her being in danger because of him.

"Just don't get us killed. Please."

"That's the goal."

As he reached the parking lot in front of the

lighthouse, he hit the brakes and jerked on the steering wheel. The car skid as it did a one-eighty.

Then he was face-to-face with the other vehicle.

Gabe held his breath as he waited to see what the driver was going to do.

AUTUMN HELD HER BREATH, unsure what was about to transpire.

Would the car ram them head-on?

She'd treated enough auto-crash victims to know the kind of damage that could inflict on the human body. She didn't want to be one of those victims.

"I don't think they're going to charge us," Gabe said beside her.

"What gives you that impression?"

"Because every death so far was made to look like an accident. There would be no way to cover this up."

That revelation brought her a small and unusual measure of comfort.

But her body didn't get the message. Her muscles remained tight and her lungs frozen as she watched and waited.

The next instant, the man in the passenger seat extended his arm out the window.

He held something in his hand.

She grabbed Gabe's bicep. "Is that a gun?"

His gaze locked on the scene. "It is. But it's not aimed at us."

"What's going on, Gabe?" Her voice cracked.

"I'm not sure. But we need to be ready for anything." He reached for the holster at his waist and drew his own gun.

Autumn sucked in a breath. She was a healer, and the thought of how many people might potentially get hurt right now left her feeling unsettled.

"I don't understand what they're doing," she said.

She expected them to aim the weapon at them. To fire. To charge the car at them.

To do *something*.

Instead, the other car sat there for another moment, gun extended out the side.

There were obviously two people in the vehicle —one behind the driver's seat and the one in the passenger seat with a gun drawn.

The next instant, a bullet pierced the air.

The car sped backward.

And a wire flew in front of them, flitting about as electricity sparked from the end.

"They shot off the powerline," Gabe muttered.

Autumn glanced over and saw a line of power poles on one side of the street.

He was right.

A live wire danced in front of them.

The cable flipped around, dangerously close to their car. It looked like a snake bent on revenge, holding all the—literal—power.

But there was no way they could go after the other car now.

Not with this wire blocking their path.

That had probably been these guys' intention the whole time.

CHAPTER SIXTEEN

GABE PUT his car in Reverse and slowly backed it away from the thrashing live wire.

When he felt confident they were a safe distance away, he picked up his phone and called Cassidy. The power company would need to come out and deal with this. But there was no way he could cross the road until it was fixed.

He didn't think those guys were coming back, but he still needed to be on guard. For that reason, he simply put down the windows and waited inside the car instead of walking toward the lighthouse.

Darkness stretched around them, and a salty breeze floated inside. When they were quiet, they could hear the waves crashing in the distance, and the lighthouse towered over them, almost as if on guard for any signs of trouble.

Gabe turned toward Autumn, ignoring the ache in his ribs as he did so. "Are you sure you're okay?"

She nodded, even though her arms still trembled. He couldn't blame her. Anybody would be scared in this situation.

"I just can't believe this is all happening." Her voice sounded softer than usual. "I just don't understand."

Without thinking, Gabe reached for her and squeezed her hand. "It's going to be okay."

Her skin felt surprisingly soft beneath his. He expected her to pull away. But she didn't. Neither did he.

Instead, their gazes caught as they sat in the car. Something passed between them.

Could Autumn share his feelings? Or was that just wishful thinking?

She seemed entirely too good for him. Too smart. Too beautiful. Too everything.

"Autumn, I—" Before he could finish his statement, his phone rang and pulled them out of the moment.

It was Colton. Maybe he had an update.

"I just heard what happened." Colton's voice rang through the car. "I'm glad that you guys are okay. Can I do anything for you?"

"I got the make of the car that was following us and the license plate," Gabe said. "I already gave it to Cassidy, but if you want to run it also, it's not a bad idea."

"Absolutely."

Gabe rattled the information off to him.

He knew better than to think that the person behind these acts would be caught easily. No doubt, the car chasing them had already been abandoned. Most likely, the vehicle had been stolen and any prints had been wiped off.

Leaving any of those clues behind would be the mark of an amateur. The person behind this was anything but.

When Gabe saw Cassidy's vehicle and one of the power company's trucks pulling onto the scene, he told Colton he'd be in touch later. He ended the call and watched as the power crew began to work. He had no idea how long he and Autumn would be here.

But at least if he was going to be stuck here, it was with Autumn.

It seemed there could be worse things.

Much, much worse things.

AUTUMN WAS grateful Gabe was with her. Of all the people she could be stuck with, Gabe was a good one.

If she'd been in the situation by herself, there was no telling what she might have done. Those men would have simply run her off the road and made her crash. Probably made it look like it had been an accident.

Was that what had happened with Dr. Johnson? Was there really a chance that these cases were somehow connected?

It seemed like a longshot. But it was definitely worth considering.

Then again, what if this wasn't about that at all? What if this was the Dimitri family coming to try to exact revenge on her?

Autumn didn't think that was the case. They were more the type to open fire than to be sneaky. In fact, they liked to make their power known.

So many questions flooded her mind.

As the power company got the situation under

control, Gabe motioned to the door. "It's probably safe to step outside now."

"That sounds great."

Autumn stepped from the vehicle and felt a cool breeze around her. The wind coming off the ocean was always remarkable, even more so right here in the area where the lighthouse was located. It was on the southern tip of the island, so the breeze swooped right from the ocean onto the waters of the Pamlico Sound.

As she stepped toward the front of the car, she felt her knees go weak. The next instant, Gabe appeared, his hands cupping her elbows. "I've got you."

She looked up at him, and her breath caught.

Yes, he did have her.

Her initial impression of the man had been so wrong. She'd just assumed that Gabe was immature, like an overgrown child with a hero complex. But even if he did have some boy-like tendencies, they weren't predominant in him.

He was capable and responsible. He truly seemed to care about the world around him, especially when it came to looking out for others.

Autumn started to open her mouth and to tell

him how much she had appreciated his strength over the past couple of days.

But before she could speak, she spotted the police chief walking toward them.

Based on the look on Cassidy's face, she had bad news.

Autumn braced for whatever was coming next.

CHAPTER SEVENTEEN

GABE KNEW when he saw Cassidy's expression that something was wrong.

"You'll be happy to know that I got the results back on that omelet," she started.

He prepared himself for what she was about to say, sensing it was bad news. "And?"

"You were right. There was rat poisoning on it."

The air left his lungs in a whoosh. Someone *had* tried to kill him.

Again.

He tried to recall any faces he'd seen at the restaurant that day. But it was no use. Everything had happened too quickly.

"Somebody must have lured you outside and

then put that poison on your food hoping . . ."
Cassidy didn't have to finish her statement.

Hoping to finish him off.

"Do you think whoever was behind this got me and Beckett outside just for that purpose?"

Cassidy frowned. "That's the other thing. Drew Crabtree said some guy paid him to discharge his weapon into the air right at that moment."

"What?" Autumn gasped beside him.

Cassidy nodded, her neck looking stiff with tension. "It took us a while to get the information out of him, but he finally told us that was what happened. The man who paid him said that nobody would get hurt, he just needed to distract his girl-friend so he could pull out an engagement ring and propose."

Gabe rubbed his jaw, feeling his muscles tight-ening until they nearly ached. "Can you describe the man?"

"The description Drew gave us was pretty unre-markable. The man was an average height and build, and he wore a baseball cap and sunglasses. Caucasian. No accent. No beard or mustache. There really wasn't much to go on. But I guess every little bit helps."

"I guess."

Cassidy nodded at the powerline as the crews worked to fix the downed wire. "I'm just glad that you weren't hurt here tonight."

"So are we." Gabe glanced at Autumn. "So are we."

AUTUMN WAS quiet as Gabe started back down the road. She was still trying to process everything that had happened.

What a whirlwind.

As she glanced at Gabe beside her, she realized that he was being unusually quiet. No doubt he also had a lot to process, especially upon learning of his friend's death.

"Would you like to talk about things?"

He cast a quick glance at her before rubbing his jaw again. "About being chased?"

"About your friend. I'm really sorry to hear what happened to him."

Gabe shook his head but kept his eyes on the road. "I just still can't believe it. Mikey was a great guy, and he was an expert hiker, among other things. I just don't think he would have fallen off of that cliff."

"Was he married?"

"Divorced. Unfortunately, it's one of the down-falls of being a SEAL."

His words washed over Autumn and made her curious about Gabe's background. "Have you been married before?"

He sent her a startled glance. "Me? No. But I was engaged. My fiancée couldn't handle the months-long deployments. That wasn't the life that she saw for her future. I guess I'm grateful that she called it off before we tied the knot."

"How long ago was that?" She knew she prob-ably shouldn't ask these kinds of questions, but she was curious. If she overstepped, she hoped Gabe would let her know.

"Three years. I suppose I poured myself into my work after that and figured that this wasn't my time for a relationship."

"I see."

Before they could talk anymore, Gabe pulled up at the clinic and stopped near her car.

Autumn hesitated as she thought about climbing inside and going back to her house. The idea was slightly terrifying. Could she swallow her pride enough to ask for help?

"If it's okay, I'm going to follow you home," Gabe said. "I'd like to make sure that you get inside okay."

It was like Gabe had read her mind. "I hate to be a bother."

His lips tugged up in a gentle, reassuring smile. "It's not a bother. I promise."

Autumn studied his expression and saw the sincerity in his gaze. Finally, she nodded. "Okay then. If you don't mind, that *would* make me feel better."

With another nod to him, she climbed out and walked to her car. But her hands trembled as she put her key into the lock.

This had shaken her up more than she'd realized. There had been a time when she didn't think anything could rattle her. But life had a way of bringing humility and making people realize they weren't as strong as they thought.

She climbed into her car and took off down the road back to her cottage. As she did, she prayed there were no surprises waiting for her there. She'd enough of those to last a lifetime it seemed.

CHAPTER EIGHTEEN

GABE'S THOUGHTS continued to race as he followed in his car behind Autumn. As he did, he scanned the road for any more signs of trouble. He didn't want to take any chances.

Because, next time, he and Autumn might not be as lucky as they had been so far.

He couldn't understand why they both seemed to have targets on their backs. The coincidence was uncanny.

He was clearly a target because he'd been a SEAL. But what about Autumn? Was she telling him the whole story? Or was there another reason why danger could be following her?

Maybe she would eventually trust Gabe enough to open up.

She'd already surprised him with what she'd told him so far. The woman was clearly his opposite —reserved, slightly bookish, professionally personable. Basically, she was the perfect mix of attributes. She was to Gabe, at least.

A few minutes later, Autumn pulled into her driveway and parked her car. Gabe pulled up beside her and climbed out of his vehicle.

"Do you mind if I check inside your house?" he called to her over the top of his car.

A fleeting smile flickered across her lips. "I was hoping you'd offer."

"You know if there's anything you need, all you have to do is ask."

Her cheeks seemed to flush at his words. She tugged a hair behind her ear as she glanced up at him. "I appreciate that."

Gabe followed behind her as she climbed the steps to her front door. But as she slipped her key into the lock, he covered her hand with his. An electric shock coursed through him at the touch, but he didn't pull back. "Do you mind?"

She released the keys into his hands and stepped back. "Go ahead."

He unlocked the door and paced into her

cottage. At once, the lovely scents of clean cotton and honeysuckle filled him.

The scents reminded him of Autumn and brought a burst of much-needed comfort. But the feeling was short-lived. This was no time to let down his guard.

With stiff muscles that were ready for action if necessary, he checked the house.

But the place was clear. No one was here. No surprises had been left.

Thankfully.

He met Autumn at the front door and handed her the keys back. "You're good to go."

"Thank you." Her stunning green eyes met his, gratitude swelling in their depths.

"It's no problem." He pointed with his gaze to his car in the distance before reluctantly saying, "I should be going."

"Of course." She nodded quickly as she stepped out of the way. But when Gabe reached the first step to depart, she called back to him. "Would you like to come inside for a minute for some coffee?"

He paused, warmth spreading through him. "I'd love some."

Another smile fluttered across her face. "Great. Come on in."

ANY ORDINARY NIGHT, Autumn might suggest sitting out on her deck and watching the sunset as they drank some coffee. Thanks to her job, she could drink the beverage at any time of the day or night. Her body seemed to be accustomed to any amount of caffeine, and the stimulant never seemed to affect her.

But, right now, the thought of being outside and exposed caused a shot of terror to wash through her. Instead, she and Gabe sat in her living room, Gabe on one side of the couch and Autumn a comfortable distance away.

She hadn't intended on inviting him inside. The words had just slipped out. But she had to admit she was happy to have him here now—for more than one reason.

Besides, she was curious to learn more about the man.

She curled her feet beneath her as she turned to him. "So, how did you become a SEAL, Gabe?"

Gabe looked into the distance before shrugging. "I guess I've always liked the thought of defending my country. But, honestly, I didn't know what I wanted to do after high school. I joined the military because I figured, why not? Turned out I was pretty good at doing what needed to get done."

"I'd say."

"I decided to see if I could get into SEAL training and BUD/S. I didn't think I would. My father's last words to me were, 'You'll never amount to anything.'" His words sounded strained. "That sentiment has stuck with me more than I'd like to admit."

Outrage shot through her as she imagined a young boy hearing those words from someone who should be the most influential person in his life. "That's terrible that your father would say that to you."

"It wasn't easy to hear, for sure." Gabe's eyes glazed as if he'd been swept back to a different time —a hard time. "But I decided to prove him wrong and see if I could get through SEAL training. It was one of the hardest things I'd ever done, and I was tempted to give up more than once. But I didn't. I made it through and knew I'd found my calling in life."

A rush of admiration shot through her. She'd heard stories about how difficult it was to become a SEAL. Only the toughest of the tough made it.

But if he'd been doing something he loved, why give it up? "Yet you're no longer a SEAL."

He shrugged, that far-off look remaining in his eyes. "That's true. But I'm still doing good, fulfilling work, and I'm doing it with men I admire and trust. Sometimes our futures don't look the way we think they should, but that's not always a bad thing. You just have to learn to go with the flow in life, I guess."

"I like the sound of that," Autumn said.

Gabe narrowed his eyes as he examined her. "Is it my turn now? Can I ask you a question?"

Autumn felt herself tense. She wasn't one of those women who considered themselves an open book. She preferred to be private when at all possible. But Gabe had shared about his life so maybe it wouldn't hurt to talk a little about herself also.

"What would you like to know?" She hoped she didn't regret asking that question.

His gaze latched onto hers, curiosity in the depths of his eyes. "Have you ever been married?"

She twisted her head, knowing she shouldn't be surprised at his question. Yet it still threw her off guard. Finally, she shook her head. "No, I've never been married. But I was engaged."

"Did you break it off? Because no guy in his right mind would call it off with you."

Her cheeks flushed. Gabe could certainly be direct. Based on the rakish smile on his face, he'd gotten just the reaction he wanted. She tugged on her collar, wishing she didn't feel so self-conscious.

"I actually caught my fiancé and my best friend together. He cheated on me."

"What?" Disbelief stretched through Gabe's voice.

Autumn shrugged. "I know people say it's hard for Navy SEALs to be married, but a lot of marriages fall apart during medical residency also. Apparently, I wasn't giving my fiancé enough attention. And that might be true. I take ownership of that. I only wish he'd decided to simply call things off instead of breaking my trust."

"That's understandable."

Autumn frowned as the memories filled her mind. "I asked my best friend, Robyn, if she would fill in for me and go look at some flowers for the wedding. She and Stanley went together. Apparently, that's when they realized they had feelings for each other. For a long time, I thought I'd set myself up."

"You should be able to trust somebody you're in a committed relationship with."

"I'd like to think so. But things didn't work out that way for me. Just like what you were saying with your former fiancée, maybe that was for the best. It's better to see somebody's true colors before you tie the knot."

"Isn't that the truth?"

They raised their coffee cups and clanked them together before sharing a smile.

Gabe stared at her another moment before looking away and setting his mug on the table. "I really should let you go. It's been a long day. For both of us."

Autumn set her mug down also and stood. "I'd hate to keep you from anything you need to do."

As he stood and strode toward the door, Autumn walked beside him. He paused and their gazes met. Autumn felt the unspoken conversations passing between them. She felt the spark. The tension of attraction.

This wasn't supposed to happen. She'd come to Lantern Beach to get away from all of that. She wanted to close her heart to any type of relationship and simply establish her career.

Did God have different plans for her?

As Stanley's face fluttered through her mind, she felt herself pull away.

She didn't want to go through that kind of hurt again. She couldn't.

Even though Gabe didn't seem like that type,

Autumn wasn't sure her heart was ready to give it a try again.

She swallowed hard before stepping back and offering a soft smile. "Thank you again for everything."

His gaze probed into hers, questions lingering there. But he kept them silent and respected her distance. "Listen, if you need anything . . ."

She nodded, maybe a little too quickly. "I'll call you."

Gabe stared at her another moment before opening the door. "Good night, Autumn."

"Good night, Gabe."

But as soon as he was gone, her place—and heart—already felt emptier.

CHAPTER NINETEEN

AUTUMN STOOD by the window and watched the taillights of Gabe's car disappear down the lane.

She hated how frightened she felt being in her cottage alone. She hadn't felt this way about the place until the past couple of days. She knew that whoever was targeting her wasn't done yet. That would be too easy.

And she'd have no peace until this person was caught.

Before she dropped the curtain, she scanned the horizon again. A small patch of woods stood across the street on an undeveloped lot. Normally, she liked the fact that she wasn't totally surrounded by houses.

But, right now, as she stared at a patch of brush, she thought she saw a red light.

A light? Was she seeing things?

She stepped back and peered between the curtain and the wall. If someone was out there, Autumn didn't want them to know she was at the window right now.

As she continued to watch, she reached for the phone in her back pocket. At the first sign that she wasn't imagining things, she needed to call Gabe. Or the police. Or both.

She could hardly breathe as she waited, as she anticipated seeing something else.

But there was nothing. Maybe everything that had happened was making her a touch paranoid. Was that it?

Most likely.

Just as she was about to step away from the window, she saw it again.

The red light.

Somebody was definitely out there, hiding in the brush in that lot.

But why would this person have a flashlight? Sure, it was dark outside. But somebody wanting to hide wouldn't turn on a light, right? And what kind of flashlight had a red light on it anyway?

That's when she realized that the beam wasn't coming from a flashlight at all.

It was the laser sight on a gun.

Just as the thought went through her mind, the glass on her window broke.

Autumn fell to the floor as her heart raced.

Someone was shooting at her.

———

AS GABE'S PHONE RANG, he glanced at the screen on his dash and saw Autumn's name. His heart skipped a beat. What was she calling about? Did she miss him already?

He silently laughed at his joke, realizing that wasn't the case. Maybe in his wildest dreams.

Instead, he pressed Talk and reminded himself to stay cool. "Hey, Autumn."

"Gabe . . ." Terror stretched through her voice. "Someone's outside my house. They're shooting at me."

His humor instantly turned into alarm. He scanned the street in front of him before jerking his wheel in a U-turn. His tires squealed and a burning scent filled the air as they skidded across the pavement.

"I'm on my way," he told her. "Get away from the window."

Through the phone line, he heard glass breaking. He heard Autumn scream.

She needed to call the police. But Gabe didn't want to end his call with her either.

"Autumn, lock yourself in an interior room," he said. "A bathroom maybe. Do you hear me?"

"Do you think this man is going to come inside and find me?" Her voice trembled with fear.

"I don't know. I don't know what he's thinking. But I need you to do that for me. I'm going to hang up and call the police. Then I'll call you right back. Okay?"

"O . . . okay." But she still sounded uncertain.

"It's going to be okay, Autumn. You hear me?"

"I do. I do."

After a moment of hesitation, Gabe ended the call. As promised, he quickly called the police then Colton. By the time those calls ended, he was back at Autumn's place.

He flinched when he saw two broken windows at the front of her house.

Was the shooter still out there? Or had he run?

Gabe climbed from his car and remained low, using the vehicle as a shield. Based on the angle of the windows, he would guess the shooter had probably been in the brush across the gravel lane.

Right now, his only goal was getting inside to check on Autumn.

But he couldn't get killed in the process.

He paused beside his car and waited, desperate to see if this guy would make any more moves.

But there was nothing.

Quickly, he dialed Autumn's number.

The phone rang and rang and rang.

She didn't pick up.

His heart rate quickened.

Had something happened to her?

He glanced at Autumn's front door. Heading up the steps with no cover would be the riskiest part of this. But he didn't have any other choice if he wanted to check on Autumn.

He said a quick prayer then took a run for the stairs, ignoring the searing pain from his fractured rib.

CHAPTER TWENTY

AUTUMN CROUCHED IN THE BATHTUB. She hated feeling like such a coward. But her fear was all too real, and she didn't know what to do about it.

So she'd followed Gabe's instructions.

She'd locked the bathroom door. Then she climbed into the bathtub, hoping the extra thick walls and pipes would protect her.

She'd also grabbed her gun from beneath the sink, but she prayed she didn't have to use it. She wanted to help heal people, not to hurt them. Yet she needed to protect herself as well.

She wanted to call Gabe. But she'd dropped her phone when she darted from the window, and the screen had shattered. Even though she grabbed the device from the floor, it was unusable.

The mistake seemed so predictable. Autumn had never seen herself as the type to make an error like that in the heat of the moment. She was an expert at dealing with emergencies, after all. But there weren't very many emergencies where she'd taken center-stage as the victim.

As she hugged her knees to her chest, she continued praying.

Dear Lord. Help me. Please. Keep Gabe safe. Help us figure out what's going on.

She froze and listened.

Everything was silent outside. She didn't hear any more gunshots. Any footsteps. Any breaking glass.

But what if the man was inside her house? What if he was slowly creeping down the hallway, only she had no clue?

The thought sent another stab of fear down her spine.

Then she heard them.

Footsteps.

Somebody was *definitely* in her house.

What was she going to do if the intruder confronted her?

She gripped her gun, still praying she wouldn't have to pull the trigger.

She remained in the bathtub with her knees pulled to her chest as she waited.

The footsteps came closer and closer.

They were heavy. Purposeful.

She pictured somebody creeping around her house. Wearing a black mask. Skulking down her hallway.

Another shiver raced through her.

As it did, a new sound filled the air.

The door handle turned. Rattled.

Whoever was here was trying to get inside.

Autumn gripped her gun and braced herself to use the weapon.

GABE PAUSED outside the bathroom door and jiggled the handle. It was locked.

"Autumn? Are you in there?"

He'd checked the rest of the house and hadn't seen her, nor had he seen the shooter. This was the only room with the door closed and locked.

He prayed Autumn was inside and that she was safe.

Movement sounded inside the room. A moment later, the door flew open and Autumn stood there.

Gone was the confident and collected doctor from the clinic. In her place was a woman shaken to her core.

Her hair was disheveled. Her gaze wavering. Her limbs trembling.

She threw herself into his arms, and Gabe held her, murmuring words of assurance into her ear. He could only imagine the fear she must have felt.

She pulled back to look him in the eyes. "Did you catch the gunman?"

"I'm nearly certain he was gone by the time I got here. But my first priority was finding you and making sure you were okay. I tried to call but . . ."

She pulled her phone from her pocket. "I can't believe I did it, but I dropped my phone, and the screen shattered."

"I'm glad that's all it was. My mind went to worst-case scenarios." He stared deeply into her gaze, trying to get a read on what was going through her head right now. "Are you sure you're okay?"

"Okay?" She raked her hand through her auburn hair and let out a shaky laugh. "I'm a nervous wreck. I'm not sure if I'd say I'm okay or not."

He kept a hand on her arm, not wanting to let her go.

As she looked up at him, something newly

vulnerable filled her gaze. "Thank you, Gabe. I'm fairly certain that when you showed up here you scared this guy off. If you hadn't come when you did . . ."

Gabe stared at Autumn, wanting nothing more than to pull her into his arms again and show her how he felt. To see if there really was something between them.

Was he imagining these feelings—both his and the ones she seemed to return? Or had the events of this week simply heightened their unreliable emotions?

He wasn't sure.

He licked his lips. "Autumn . . ."

Her gaze locked with his. "Yes?"

"I just want you to know . . ."

Before he could finish his statement, someone barged into the house.

"Police!"

Backup had arrived.

Gabe frowned.

And right at the wrong time.

CHAPTER TWENTY-ONE

AUTUMN INSISTED on sleeping at the clinic that night. Gabe offered to let her crash at an empty apartment on the Blackout campus, but she wasn't ready for that yet.

Maybe she was being foolish. But she needed to feel like she still had some control of her life. Besides, she had a small office at the clinic, complete with a couch where she could sleep.

The police had stationed someone outside her door. Chief Chambers had told her that the officer would remain there at least through the next day just in case Autumn had more trouble.

She did feel better knowing that somebody was out there. Part of her wished it was Gabe. But then he wouldn't get any sleep, and he needed to rest after everything that had happened. Apparently, keeping her alive was more than a one-person job. She needed a whole team.

That thought didn't make her feel any better.

Autumn was surprised at how refreshed she felt, even after the restless night. Her brain was wired as she thought through everything that had happened.

The more she thought about it, the more she wondered about the gas that was sprayed on the SEAL team on that mission. She thought about the symptoms Gabe had listed for each of them. Thought about the research that Dr. Johnson had been doing.

His assistant was supposed to be sending it to her, and Autumn couldn't wait to see the details for herself.

Until then, there was one thing she wanted to do: She wanted to examine each of the Blackout guys herself.

She wasn't sure if they would go for it. But she wanted to make a record of their symptoms and their vitals. Do a blood test on each of them. Look for commonalities.

These guys deserved to know the truth about what had happened to them while they were serving their country. Anything otherwise would be a disservice to them.

Now she just needed to convince them that that was what they should do.

AS GABE SAT at his desk, his phone rang. His heart skipped a beat when he saw it was the Lantern Beach Medical Clinic. Was Autumn calling?

He cleared his throat before answering. "Hello?"

"Hey, Gabe. It's Autumn. I hope I'm not catching you at a bad time, but I have a question for you."

Autumn sounded normal, like she'd put last night's events behind her. The thought both comforted him and made him worry. She couldn't let her guard down too easily.

He leaned back in his chair, glad for the distraction. "What's going on?"

"How do you think the rest of your team would feel about me running some tests on them?"

He raised his eyebrows, not expecting that question. "Tests? Like lab rats kind of things?"

She let out a quick chuckle. "No, not like that at all. I'd like to take everyone's vitals, as well as some bloodwork. I'd like to figure out what you were sprayed with."

"I appreciate your concern, but it's like I said—our doctor checked us out and didn't find anything of concern."

"I know, and I'm not saying your doctor was incompetent. I'm just saying I think it would be wise to have a second set of eyes on those findings."

Gabe thought about her request a moment before slowly nodding. It seemed reasonable enough. "Will you need to examine me also?"

"If you're okay with it. Even though I already have some blood samples, I'd like to run the same tests on everyone."

"Understandable. I'll talk to the guys and see what they say. How does that sound?"

"Perfect. Thank you."

He ended the call and leaned back in his chair. He'd catch the rest of the guys in a minute. Right now, he wanted to examine everything he knew about this case so far.

Gabe started by putting together a list of all the crimes as they had occurred.

First, he was injured in a hit-and-run.

Next, somebody broke into Autumn's apartment.

Then, Autumn was sprayed in the face with an unknown substance, most likely chloroform.

Rat poisoning was left on Gabe's food.

He and Autumn had been chased and faced a downed powerline.

Someone had shot at Autumn at her house last night.

Gabe stared at the list and shook his head. What exactly was going on here?

He didn't know. And he didn't like it.

Right now, Mario Dimitri was his best guess as to whom the culprit was. Gabe had pulled up the man's picture on his phone and memorized his dark hair, meaty arms, and various tattoos. The most noticeable one was an oversized lion on the man's left bicep. The image seemed to dare anyone to defy him.

The fact that the man's whereabouts were unknown bothered Gabe.

In some circumstances, he could call one of his contacts and ask for help in pinging someone's phone number. Gabe couldn't do it himself, not without a warrant and law enforcement on his side.

But Gabe didn't think his contact would go for it in this matter—not without more compelling evidence.

A few minutes later, Gabe glanced at his watch and stood. He was going to go out on the island and ask around to some people he knew. Maybe someone had seen this Mario guy. His burly appearance would make him stand out.

Before leaving, Gabe stuck his head in the conference room. The rest of his team was there talking about an upcoming case. "Hey, guys. I have a question."

"What's going on?" Rocco looked up from his computer.

He told them about Autumn's idea and then waited for their reaction.

Finally, Rocco spoke. "I don't mind. I've always wondered what that substance was. Maybe more tests will give us more answers."

"Same here," Axel said.

"I'm in," Beckett said.

"Great," Gabe nodded. "I'll let Autumn know."

"I'm sure you will." Axel raised his eyebrows and grinned.

Gabe narrowed his gaze at his friend. "This was her idea not mine."

"Let's make a wager on how long it will take Gabe to ask Autumn out," Beckett said. "I'm guessing four days. Anyone in?"

"I say a week," Axel added.

"You're all wrong," Rocco said. "Two days or less."

Gabe's scowl deepened. "You guys are so funny. Really, you are."

"We're just trying to look out for you, Junior." Beckett winked.

"Now, our next wager can be on whether or not she's going to say yes . . ." Axel said before hearty chuckles filled the room.

Gabe wanted to deny his words. But that was the million-dollar question.

CHAPTER TWENTY-TWO

GABE MADE his rounds through town, stopping at all his favorite places to show Mario's picture to anybody he knew. So far, no one had recognized the guy. He wasn't ready to give up yet though. He still had a few more stops to make.

Times like this, he had to think his chattiness might pay off. He was the type who was known to start up conversations with strangers at any given moment. He figured that would either get him far in life or totally hinder him.

Right now, he'd use it to his advantage.

As he made his way down the boardwalk that stretched the resort area of the island, he stepped inside Peyton's Pastries, the newest dessert shop here on the island.

Peyton Ellison was dating Rocco, and the woman was just as sweet as the desserts she made. And Rocco was as happy as a clam to have her so close. The rest of the island, meanwhile, was thankful for her cupcakes.

Peyton greeted Gabe with a wide grin as he stepped inside. "Gabe. What brings you here?"

The scents of chocolate, cinnamon, and vanilla filled his senses. "I'd like to get two of your Decadent Double Chocolate cupcakes, for starters."

Her eyebrows shot up as curiosity filled her gaze. "Two?"

He shrugged. He figured he might bring a treat to Autumn later. Cupcakes always cheered people up, right? But he didn't need to tell Peyton that, especially not when he considered the bet the guys made concerning him and Autumn.

He knew for certain that if he did ask Autumn out, he wouldn't be telling his team about it.

"I must be especially hungry today or maybe my sweet tooth is kicking in." Gabe rubbed his shoulder, that familiar ache pulsating there. Between that, his ribs, and the general soreness from his accident, he felt decades older than he actually was.

"I understand that." Peyton slipped on a plastic glove before heading to the display and pulling out two of her chocolate cupcakes. She placed them in a box and slid them across the counter to him. "These are on me."

"You don't have to do that."

"I know I don't." She winked. "But I want to."

"Thank you, Peyton. I appreciate it."

She leaned on the counter as she turned toward him. "Now, was there another reason you came in here? I know you Blackout guys. You always have an ulterior motive."

She had him there.

"Actually, there is." Gabe pulled up Mario's picture on his phone and held it so she could see. "Have you seen this guy in town, by chance?"

As soon as Peyton looked at the picture, her eyes widened. "Actually, I have. He was just in here two hours ago."

Gabe's pulse quickened. "Is that right? Are you sure?"

"I remember that tattoo on his arm. It's hard to forget a lion like that."

"Did you hear him say anything while he was in here?"

Peyton frowned before nodding. "He said he needed to check into his rental, but he still had another hour to kill."

"Did he say where his rental was?"

She let out a sigh as her gaze wandered to the left in recall. "I think he said he's staying at a house named Ocean Breeze. He asked if I knew where it was. But I'm too new in town to remember all the house names. I wasn't much help."

"Actually, you've been a ton of help." Gabe took a step back. "Thank you, Peyton." He held up his cupcakes. "For everything."

"No problem." She waved to him as he slipped out the door.

He had a lead.

Now he needed to check it out.

AS AUTUMN SAT at her desk, she picked up her new phone.

Gabe had dropped it by earlier since she'd smashed her old one. He'd taken the sim card from her old phone and placed it into the new one. All her old contacts and numbers had transferred over.

She hated to be a pest, but she couldn't seem to let this go. She dialed Sarah Andrews' number. The woman picked up on the third ring.

"Sarah, this is Autumn Spenser again."

"Oh, hi, Autumn." The woman's voice seemed to sink with disappointment when she said Autumn's name.

"I'm not trying to be a pest," she started. "But I was wondering if you'd had a chance to send out the research Dr. Johnson was working on yet?"

"It's funny you asked that because I sat down to do that this morning. But when I got on his computer, all the research files were gone."

Autumn bristled. Certainly, she hadn't heard Sarah correctly. "What?"

"It's true." Sarah let out a long sigh. "I have no idea what's going on, but the research is gone. Every single page of it."

Autumn's mind raced through possibilities, raced to find a reason. "When was the last time Dr. Johnson worked on it on his computer?"

"He was working on it the night he died. I have a hard time believing he deleted all his research before he left that evening."

So did Autumn.

A bad feeling swirled in her gut. "No, that doesn't sound right, does it?"

"Not at all," Sarah said. "I'm still trying to go through everything to see if I can recover the files."

"Is anything else missing?"

"Not that I can tell—not that I'm an expert on how his computer looked. But it seems like everything is still there except this research."

Autumn knew what that meant. Somebody had either physically snuck onto his computer and deleted it, or they'd hacked into his cloud account and deleted it that way.

Autumn thanked Sarah and ended the call.

But as she leaned back into her chair, unease continued to grow inside her.

Whatever Dr. Johnson had been working on, somebody didn't want Autumn—or anyone else—to see it.

Was that what all these crimes against her led back to?

She frowned.

She wasn't sure. But that was her best guess.

CHAPTER TWENTY-THREE

AFTER MAKING A FEW PHONE CALLS, Gabe found the house he was looking for. He stopped before he reached Ocean Breeze and parked his car a few houses down. He didn't want to announce his arrival so easily, didn't want to give the man a heads-up.

Gabe had already called Beckett, and his teammate was on his way here now. Gabe knew not to try to handle a situation like this by himself if not absolutely necessary.

As he stood near his car, he stared at the house in the distance. It was one of the smaller ones on the street. One story and pale blue with a wraparound deck. The place was only two lots back from the ocean and probably much more affordable than the large three-story houses all around.

From where Gabe stood, he saw a car in the driveway with Maryland plates.

This had to be their guy.

It couldn't be a coincidence that the man was here right now.

Finally, Beckett pulled up behind him. His friend started toward him and nodded toward the house in the background. "This is it?"

Gabe nodded. "This is it. Are we ready to have a talk with this guy and see what he's doing here?"

"There's no better time than the present," Beckett said.

Since they weren't official law enforcement here on the island, they would need to be careful. Still, there was nothing wrong with having a little heart-to-heart talk with this guy.

But Gabe's muscles were poised to fight if it came down to it.

They climbed the steps and knocked at the door.

They waited several minutes, but no one answered.

Beckett knocked again, pounding harder than before.

This time, footsteps sounded inside.

A moment later, the door opened and Mario Dimitri stood there, a towel at his waist and his hair wet.

He scowled with reprehension as he stared at the two of them. "Can't a man take a shower?"

That hadn't been the reaction Gabe expected. Hostility? Yes. But this all seemed a little too casual.

"Mario Dimitri, we have a few questions for you," Gabe started.

The man narrowed his eyes, water dripping from his hair and down his chest. "Who are you?"

"We're with the private security firm Blackout."

A wall instantly formed over his gaze. "What do you want to talk to me about?"

The man sounded truly perplexed.

"Autumn Spenser," Beckett said.

The man stepped back, recognition suddenly filling his gaze. "I don't know who you're talking about."

Gabe bristled. The man's denial only made him look guilty. "I think you do. We can do this the easy way or the hard way."

The man grunted, almost sounding amused at the thought of taking on Gabe and Beckett. "And what's the hard way?"

"Bringing the police into this," Beckett said. "What's your choice?"

Mario stared at them another moment before finally nodding toward his living room. "Fine, fine. Come in."

They stepped into the cottage, but both remained on guard. There was no telling if this would turn ugly or not. But at least they'd gotten this far.

Mario didn't offer them a seat, so instead they stood in the center of the room.

"What do you want to know?" Mario demanded, tightening the white towel around his waist.

Gabe latched his gaze onto Mario's. "We know you're the one who's been threatening Autumn Spenser."

"Whoa, whoa, whoa." Mario waved his hands in the air. "I haven't been threatening nobody."

"You don't think that we're going to believe your presence here is a coincidence, do you?" Gabe asked. "Especially since you have a clear vendetta against Dr. Spenser."

Mario ran a hand over his face. "You don't know what you're talking about."

"What we know is that someone has made an

attempt on her life more than once this week. You're the most likely suspect."

"You know what?" Beckett pulled out his phone. "Maybe it's a good idea to give the police a call after all."

"Wait!" Mario leaned toward them, nearly losing his towel. He grabbed it and pulled it back up again. "It's not like that."

"Then what is it like?" Beckett demanded, still holding his phone, poised to make a call.

"I did come here because of Autumn, but not because I want to kill her." Mario sliced a hand through the air to drive home his point.

"What did you want to do?" Gabe heard the anger simmering in his voice. He was tired of playing these games. He just wanted answers.

"I wanted to make it clear to her that nobody messes with the Dimitri family."

Gabe narrowed his eyes. "And that's why you broke into her house? Why you shot at her?"

"Shot at her?" Mario's voice climbed with confusion. "What? No. I didn't do that."

"I find that hard to believe." Gabe crossed his arms, his impatience growing by the moment.

"Look, I can prove it wasn't me. I just got into town today."

"That's what you're saying," Gabe said. "But your presence and timing here are uncanny."

"I *did* just get into town, and I have a lot of credit card receipts to prove it. I've been hitting the casinos in Atlantic City. Told the wife it was a business trip. I just got here on the island today. A few hours ago, as a matter of fact."

That matched what Peyton had said, but Gabe wasn't ready to totally believe him yet. "Why did you come here? How exactly did you want to make your disappointment clear to Dr. Spenser?"

He narrowed his eyes, probably realizing how bad this looked. "I just wanted her to see me. To know that I was still thinking about what happened. To let her know I still blame her."

"And that's it?" Gabe asked. "Seems a little fishy to me."

"Look, I haven't always been a good guy. But I definitely didn't try to kill her."

"With your record, I find that hard to believe."

Mario looked at Gabe, his eyes narrowing as a small growl rumbled from deep inside him. "I'm not that person anymore."

Gabe raised his chin. "The fact that you're here to intimidate her says otherwise."

Mario stared at him another moment before breaking his gaze and shaking his head. He seemed like a tough guy, but he wasn't—not when push came to shove.

"Look, I'll prove it," Mario said. "Just let me grab my phone."

Gabe watched as Mario walked to the kitchen counter and picked up the device. He punched in a few things before showing them the screen. Sure enough, all his receipts confirmed he'd been up in Atlantic City.

"Now do you believe me?" Mario's voice rose as he stared at them, a hopeful expression in his gaze.

It *did* appear the man had an alibi. But Gabe wasn't ready to let him off the hook yet.

"What about your older brother, Lucas?" Gabe demanded. "Could he be in town and behind everything happening?"

Just as he asked the question, he heard a click behind him.

Felt a shadow.

Someone was here.

Someone holding a gun.

AUTUMN FINISHED RECORDING Rocco Foster's vitals. She'd already taken a sample of his blood that she'd send off. She'd listened to his heartbeat, taken his temperature, listed his symptoms, and tested his reflexes. That wasn't to mention the fact that she'd asked him more questions than she could count. She wanted to cover all her bases.

When she finished, she stepped back and offered a polite smile. "Thanks for coming in. I appreciate you letting me do this."

He pulled his shirt down and nodded before his British accent filled the room. "I think I can speak for each of us when I say we'd all love some answers. Something about what happened has never sat right with me."

She crossed her arms and leaned back against the desk in her exam room. "And rightly so. It's all very strange. If it was a nerve agent, I just don't understand why it would be having this effect on you."

"Hopefully, these blood samples might be able to tell you something."

"Let's hope so."

Rocco stood and paused. "Listen, I'm sorry to hear about everything you're going through."

His words caused a knot to form in Autumn's throat. "It's certainly been unexpected. I don't know how you guys live like this all the time."

He shrugged. "I'd like to say you get used to it, but you don't."

"I've been very thankful to have Gabe around. He's been a real godsend."

A smile tugged at Rocco's lips. "He's a good guy. Chatty. Eager to learn. But he's also tough, and sometimes I actually get a little jealous of his enthusiasm."

She fought a smile at the statement. Rocco's words pretty much fit Gabe to a T. "I think it's pretty amazing how he's risen above his background to get to where he is today."

"Pretty amazing. That's a good way to put it." Rocco stepped through the door. "How about if I send Axel in next? Don't be surprised if he gives you some insight into Gabe also."

"You guys really like to pick at each other, don't you?"

"It's what we do best." Amusement caught his voice.

"I thought protecting people was what you did best."

He shrugged. "That too. I'll see you later, Dr. Spenser. Thank you for everything you're doing."

She nodded as she watched him walk away.

She hoped she could offer these guys some answers. They deserved them. And so did Dr. Johnson.

CHAPTER TWENTY-FOUR

"LUCAS?" Mario's voice rose. "What are you doing here? What's with the gun?"

"What am *I* doing here? What are *you* doing here? Who are *they*?"

Gabe stole a glance behind him and saw Mario's older brother standing there with a gun pointed at them.

"Put your hands in the air." Lucas sneered at them.

Beckett and Gabe glanced at each other. Right now, they would comply. But they could take this guy out in two seconds flat. Gabe had no doubt about that.

Despite that, they raised their hands, playing this on his terms—for now.

"We're just here asking questions." Beckett's voice sounded as even and calm as his controlled movements.

"Questions about what?" Lucas demanded, his eyes narrow with distrust.

"They're asking about Byron." Mario tightened his towel again.

"What about him?" Spittle flew from Lucas' mouth as he asked the question.

"We want to know if you guys came here to try to kill the doctor who failed to diagnosis his aneurysm in time," Gabe said, filling in the blanks.

Lucas' gaze darkened as his hulking figure filled the space—along with his scowl. "And what if we are?"

"Lucas . . ." Mario's voice contained warning.

"I don't know who these clowns are. I don't have to say nothing to them."

"These guys are private security agents," Mario explained. "They think that we're trying to hurt Dr. Spenser."

"She deserves to be hurt," Lucas said. "Especially after her failure."

"Lucas . . . you're not doing yourself any favors." Mario's voice held a warning. "We agreed to stay below the radar. Don't you remember?"

"I don't have to do anything I don't want to do," Lucas said. "But right now, I do know what I want. I want to smack the smug looks off of these guys' faces."

"Look." Gabe knew he needed to subdue the charge in the air before this turned ugly. "We're not here to cause trouble. We just want to know why you're here."

"Why *are* you here?" Mario asked his brother.

Lucas stared at Mario, a dumbfounded expression on his face. "I'm here because Pippy thinks you're running around on her. I came to check it out. Didn't expect to see you here with these two."

"Pippy sent you down here?" Mario repeated.

If Gabe remembered correctly, Pippy was Mario's wife.

"Somebody called this week, saying he was from a Mercedes dealership. She thought maybe you had a mistress and that it was her husband calling to snoop for more information."

Mario's mouth dropped open as he shook his head. "Pippy's got to know I'd never cheat on her. I love her too much."

"This is a really great and touching conversation," Gabe said. "How about we put the gun away?"

"Did I ask you?" Lucas pointed the gun at him again as he sneered again.

"We just want to make sure that our friend Dr. Spenser is safe," Beckett said.

Gabe held his breath.

This could go one of two ways: it could get really ugly or they could walk away.

He waited to see what it was going to be.

AFTER AUTUMN FINISHED EXAMINING AXEL, she sat at her desk and took a sip of water.

Somebody knocked at her open office door, and she looked over to see Hannah Welborn, one of the clinic nurses, standing there.

"You got something in the mail." Hannah stepped inside and handed her a thick manila envelope. "I had to sign for it so I wanted to hand it to you personally."

"Thank you."

Autumn took the envelope and asked Hannah to close the door behind her.

There was no return address on the envelope so Autumn tore the seal, being extra cautious as she remembered the spray that had come from her lunchbox. Had someone sent her some type of substance in this envelope? Was that the reason that there was no return address?

She needed to be careful until she knew more.

She slid the papers from the envelope onto her desk.

But when she saw the handwritten note on the front page, her eyes welled with tears.

This was from Dr. Johnson.

DEAR AUTUMN,

I have been working on some research for the past two years. I'm getting closer to answers, but the more facts I uncover, the more strange things have been occurring in my life. I think that somebody wants me dead. That's why I'm sending this to you.

I got your voicemail, and I'll look into what you said. But I find the timing suspicious because I think what you're saying could be related to my research.

I printed some of it, and I'm mailing it to you because I don't trust that my computer is safe, nor do I trust any digital correspondence.

I hope you can sort through this and make

sense of it. That if something happens to me maybe you can even finish the work I have started.

You know I've always admired you and your work. You're one smart lady, and, if anyone can figure this out, it's you.

Best of luck,

Dr. Johnson

AUTUMN'S HEART pounded in her ears. Dr. Johnson had sent this the night she'd left that voice-mail. That meant he'd sent this the night he died. Probably right before his car accident.

Had his death even been an accident?

He'd thought somebody wanted him dead.

She hated to think he'd been murdered.

She set the note aside and began flipping through the pages. It was going to take a while to look through everything and to try to figure out what it all meant.

But at least she might find some answers from this. That was an answer to prayer.

As she leaned back in her chair, ready to dive in, her phone rang.

An unknown number popped up on her screen.

Could it be one of the guys from Blackout? Quickly, she answered.

Instead, a deep voice said, "You should have minded your own business."

CHAPTER TWENTY-FIVE

"LOOK, I *am* upset with Dr. Spenser, but I'm not trying to hurt her." Lucas shrugged and looked at Gabe and Beckett like they were the crazy ones. "Really, I wouldn't mind a nice cash settlement payout from her insurance. Can you blame me?"

"So you're not trying to kill her?" Gabe didn't bother to hide the doubt from his voice as he stared Lucas down. This guy was a punk and a hothead. He wouldn't put anything past him.

Lucas shoved his gun into his waistband and took a step back as if in an effort to make peace. "No, I'm not trying to kill her. I miss my brother every day. And I *did* blame that doctor for what happened for a long time. But she seemed sincerely sorry over his death."

"You really just came here to spy on me?" Mario's voice rose as an incredulous tone captured every word.

"I did. When I saw these two come in, I got worried. I thought you were in trouble."

Gabe let out a sigh, not prepared—or desiring—to deal with these two right now. "When exactly did you get into town?"

"I followed Mario in on the ferry. I was going to shadow him for a while. Then I saw you two were here. You kind of messed up my plans." He turned his gaze back to Mario. "You're not here to meet someone else are you, bro?"

"You know me better than that. I love my Pippy." Mario tapped his heart as if to drive home his words.

"That's what I told her." Lucas sounded skeptical over the whole thing also.

Gabe and Beckett glanced at each other. They could probably check the most recent ferry information and verify that these guys had just arrived, but Gabe's gut told him that they weren't the culprits here.

But if not them, then who?

They excused themselves before stepping outside and walking down the lane back to their vehicles.

"I was halfway hoping that it would be them," Beckett muttered.

Gabe frowned. "Me too."

This had been their best lead yet, but it didn't look like it would pan out.

"I say we get to the clinic and see if there are any updates there," Beckett said.

Gabe nodded. Any chance to see Autumn sounded like an opportunity he didn't want to miss.

AUTUMN STARTLED when she sensed a shadow in her doorway. She looked up from the papers she'd been studying and spotted Beckett and Gabe standing at the entry to her office.

Gabe shrugged as he observed her, that warm look simmering in his gaze as he apologized. "We didn't mean to scare you. Is this a bad time?"

She pulled off her reading glasses and shook her head. "No, not at all. Come in."

Gabe and Beckett stepped inside and closed the door behind them before taking the seats across from her desk. She was glad to see them. That phone call had startled her.

The caller had just told her she should have

minded her own business, and then the line had gone dead.

"We have an update for you," Gabe started.

She put thoughts of the phone call aside. There would be time to tell them about it later. She wanted to hear their update first.

He proceeded to tell her about their meeting with Mario and Lucas. She felt her eyes widen with every new detail.

Finally, as they finished, she shook her head and pinched the skin between her eyes. "I can't believe this. Do you think they're telling the truth?"

"We'll double-check their story," Beckett said. "But my instincts tell me that they were being honest. Plus, Mario told Peyton at the bakery that he'd just arrived in town."

Autumn leaned back in her chair and shook her head as she processed the update. "I can't believe the two of them came here. They just want to intimidate me, don't they?"

"That's how it seems." Gabe frowned with recognizable regret.

Autumn let out a sigh before leaning toward her desk and picking up the manila envelope. "I have an update for you two also. I got the information about

Dr. Johnson's research in the mail today. He must have sent it right before his car accident."

Gabe's eyes widened. "Is that right? Have you been able to find any ties with what's going on?"

She frowned, trying to ignore the overwhelmed feeling that wanted to consume her. She hadn't realized how much pressure she'd feel at the task or the burden of everything that had happened.

"It's a lot to go through, and I'm still trying to make sense of things," she said. "But I'm getting closer and closer."

"That's good news at least."

She swallowed hard, knowing this conversation wasn't done yet. "I also got a threatening phone call. Someone told me that I should have minded my own business."

Gabe stared at her, his expression pensive. "That's all he said?"

She nodded.

"This person isn't backing off, is he?" Beckett said.

"No, he's not." Autumn frowned.

"I wanted to let you know that I put in a call with my friend who's a state patrol officer to ask about Dr. Johnson's death," Gabe said. "He assured me that he's looking at the accident report and will get back with me. I asked him to do it in a timely fashion if possible. So I'm hoping to hear back from him soon."

Gratitude filled her. "I really do appreciate all you guys are doing for me."

"Did you get the information you needed from the rest of the team?" Beckett leaned back in the chair, taking in the conversation.

"From Rocco and Axel. I just need to collect some information, samples, vitals from the two of you also."

Gabe stood. "Why don't I let Beckett go first? I need to make a phone call anyway."

"Everything okay?" Beckett's gaze flickered with curiosity.

"I just want to call Brandon and make sure that he's all right."

Beckett's eyes clouded with concern. "Good idea."

With one more nod to Autumn, Gabe stepped out into the hallway.

Autumn watched him leave, part of her glad that he was going last. Because maybe that would give her a little more time with him at the end.

More time with him? What had gotten into her?

It wasn't like her. Even when she'd been engaged to Stanley, she didn't remember pining over him like this. It was silly.

But that didn't change the fact that she was looking forward to getting to know Gabe more.

CHAPTER TWENTY-SIX

"WHAT DO you mean Mikey is dead?" Brandon said.

Gabe leaned back against the wall with his phone to his ear as he stood in the clinic hallway outside of the exam room. He didn't want to leave—not when he could keep an eye on things here.

"I'm sorry to be the one to have to break this to you," he told his friend. "But Mikey's body was found yesterday. It appears he fell off a cliff."

"Fell off a cliff?" Brandon's voice climbed with surprise. "There's no way Mikey fell off a cliff."

Even though Brandon couldn't see him, Gabe nodded, finding comfort in their shared opinion. "My thoughts exactly."

"It's true, isn't it?" Disbelief stretched through

Brandon's voice. "People from our team are being killed off one by one."

A lump formed in Gabe's throat at the thought of it. "Have you received any threats or had any weird incidents happen to you lately?"

"Not lately. But I'll definitely be keeping my eyes wide open."

That was good news, at least. "It appears that I'm the one they're concentrating on right now. I've had a couple of incidents that have left me feeling pretty uneasy."

"I guess we all need to watch our backs, huh?"

"I'd say so." It was a reality he didn't want to live with, but he apparently didn't have a choice right now—not if he wanted to stay alive. "I just wanted to call and give you that update. Watch yourself."

"Got it. You too. I hope that we'll be able to get together for that camping trip soon. I've already asked for time off from the dealership."

"I'll make it happen." Gabe only hoped they all survived long enough to do so. But he kept that thought quiet.

At the end of the call, he shoved his phone back in his pocket and glanced around. A couple of people milled around in the waiting area. Some nurses walked back and forth from the rooms. A TV sounded from one of the rooms, and he heard people talking farther down the hallway.

But nothing suspicious caught his eye. Gabe was sure that wouldn't last for long. Danger seemed to be around every corner.

He leaned against the wall and crossed his arms, waiting for Beckett to finish.

So, if he could rule out the Dimitri family as people who have potentially been trying to hurt Autumn, then who did that leave?

The next logical conclusion was that it was somebody associated with Dr. Johnson's research. Had someone known that the doctor mailed the information to Autumn?

What if they had followed Dr. Johnson to the post office, seen him mail it, and that's when the man had been run off the road? Because that was what Gabe suspected had happened. Somebody had most likely run the man down, just like they had tried to run Gabe down.

If his timeline was correct, then the night Dr. Johnson mailed that letter was the same night someone had broken into Autumn's place. But one person couldn't be in two places.

Did that mean that there were two people involved?

Two people . . . it was the only thing that made sense given everything that had happened.

But if two people were involved, then it only made sense in Gabe's mind that somebody would have needed to hire them. Because the guys behind these acts seemed to know what they were doing. They seemed to be professionals.

Gabe's spine tightened at the thought.

Before he could think about it any longer, the door behind him opened and Beckett stepped out.

He glanced behind him at Autumn and muttered, "Gabe's all yours."

Gabe's breath caught as he looked at Autumn. He knew their meeting was only professional.

So why was he looking forward to it so much?

AS AUTUMN LISTENED to Gabe's heartbeat, her mind raced. She had a lot to think about, to say the least. And now she was finding herself being distracted by the strangely alluring scent of Gabe's spicy cologne.

"So you haven't had time to fully comprehend the scope of what Dr. Johnson was researching?" Gabe asked as he breathed in and out, in and out.

He'd raised his shirt up and had taken off his baseball cap. His muscular back stared back at her, complete with at least three scars.

Autumn moved the stethoscope on his back. She didn't say anything for a moment as she listened to his heartbeat.

Finally, she pulled the stethoscope down and wrapped it behind her neck. "I wish I could say I'd made sense of it, but it's clear that when Dr. Johnson sent me this information, he simply gave me everything he had without taking the time to organize his thoughts. It's going to take a while for me to sort through his notes."

"I understand." Disappointment filled his voice.

Autumn paused and lowered herself onto a stool in front of Gabe, her gaze locking with his. "What are you thinking?"

She knew she was probably sitting too close and that she should back away. But this wasn't an official checkup. Gabe was here as a friend. Maybe that's why she didn't scoot back when their knees brushed.

His gaze glanced down to where their legs touched, almost as if he'd felt a shock of electricity also. Then he pulled his gaze back up to meet hers, some new emotion simmering in the depths of his eyes.

He swallowed hard before saying, "I believe there are at least two people involved with everything that's going on."

"But we still have no idea who those people are, correct?"

"My only guess is that it's someone who doesn't want you to see this research."

She crossed her arms, her thoughts still racing. "You mean like the person behind the gas being sprayed on you?"

His pupils widened. "Either the person who was behind spraying it or maybe even the person who developed it. If the substance didn't appear on the radar of any military personnel, then maybe it's a new chemical that's being developed. Maybe Dr. Johnson's death was to keep this under wraps."

Autumn frowned, chewing on that idea. She didn't like the implications, but Gabe's idea might have merit. "It's an interesting theory, but how would Dr. Johnson have discovered it?"

Gabe's gaze locked with hers, the blue of his eyes mesmerizing. "That's a good question, and I wish he was around so that we could ask him. In your line of work, do people ever send you bizarre or unsolvable medical cases?"

Autumn looked away before Gabe saw too many

unspoken emotions in her expression. She needed to keep things professional here. "Sometimes. So you think that maybe somebody sent Dr. Johnson this information and asked for his help, not knowing what they were getting him into?"

Gabe shrugged. "The timing is strange. That Dr. Johnson just happened to be researching this and then you happened to run into us."

Autumn crossed her arms and frowned. "I agree. I usually don't believe in coincidences but . . ." A shiver ran through her.

His blue eyes implored hers again. "I know Dillinger is stationed right outside, but I'd be happy to stay here and keep an eye on you."

THE SINCERITY in his voice touched her—maybe even thrilled her. But she tried not to let that show. "I know. But what I really want is for you to find the person doing this. I know I can't hire you. I know I'm not an official client, but—"

Gabe leaned forward and touched her hand, sending another round of sparks through her blood.

"Getting paid for this is the least of my concerns," he said. "I just want to know that you're going to be safe."

Something about the way Gabe said the words made Autumn believe he really did care about her. That realization sent a flood of warmth through her.

Falling for somebody now was a bad, bad idea. Concentrating on her career and her new life here in Lantern Beach would be the smartest thing to do.

So why did her heart want to argue with her?

CHAPTER TWENTY-SEVEN

GABE NEEDED to get back to headquarters so he could continue working on this case.

Before he left, he paused in front of Autumn to tell her goodbye. As he did, he felt himself being drawn toward her. All he wanted was to step closer. To feel her hair under his fingertips. To catch a whiff of her wildflower perfume.

It had been all he could do to contain himself as he felt her hands on his back earlier. As she'd leaned toward him during the checkup, her face only inches from his. He knew there was nothing romantic about an exam. But he couldn't deny the sparks he felt.

"When work is over, will you call me?" Gabe asked. "Especially in light of everything that's happened, I'd like to make sure myself that you get safely to wherever you're going, whether that's back to your cottage or somewhere else."

She stared at him a moment before nodding. "That sounds like the smart thing to do. I'll call you. I'm guessing I have only a couple hours of work left before I leave. Will that work?"

"Of course it will. Whatever you need, I'll make it happen."

Something flashed in her gaze. Surprise? Delight? He wasn't sure.

After a moment of hesitation, Gabe stepped back. Reluctantly, he began walking to his car. He would get whatever it was he needed to do done and then come back here to make sure Autumn was okay.

On his way out, he passed Dillinger and gave him a nod. He knew the man would do a good job keeping Autumn safe. He was a former SEAL himself.

Gabe climbed in his car and slammed the door. But as he did, he looked at the seat beside him and drew in a quick breath.

A snake coiled beneath a sweatshirt he'd left there—coiled except for his head, which rose toward Gabe.

This wasn't just any snake.

It was a black mamba—the deadliest snake in the world.

———

AUTUMN GLANCED at the floor and saw Gabe's baseball cap. If she hurried, she could still catch him.

She grabbed it and darted down the hall. But as soon as she ran out of the front doors, Dillinger called her. "Dr. Spenser?"

"I need to give this to Gabe," she called over her shoulder. "He left it."

"Let me walk with you. I promised I wouldn't let you out of my sight."

Autumn knew better than to argue. Dillinger hurried to catch up with her as she paused in the parking lot. Her gaze scanned the cars around her until she saw Gabe's.

Good. He was still here.

In fact, it didn't even appear he'd started his car yet.

Moving with less urgency now, she and Dillinger made their way toward his vehicle. But the closer Autumn got, the more she realized something didn't make sense. She could barely see

Gabe's silhouette in the car, but he remained unmoving.

Why was he just sitting there? It didn't even appear that he had his phone to his ear.

She went to his passenger side and started to knock on the window when some kind of internal instinct stopped her.

Gabe sat dead still staring out the front window. Even when Autumn had approached the car, he didn't look at her.

That wasn't like him. He was the type who always noticed everything going on around him. So what was wrong?

When her gaze traveled to the passenger seat, she froze.

A snake coiled there. The nope rope, as her mom had called them, stared right at Gabe, poised to strike.

Autumn took a step back, trying not to get the snake agitated.

"Dillinger . . ."

"What's going on?" He paused behind her.

"It's a snake. In Gabe's car."

He stepped beside her and peered inside. As he did, he sucked in a quick breath. "If I'm not mistaken, that's a black mamba."

"A black mamba?" Gabe had told Autumn that story about the snake he'd encountered in Africa.

It wasn't a coincidence that very snake was in his car right now. What had he said? That it was one of the deadliest snakes in the world?

Autumn remembered her medical school training. They'd covered treating venomous snake bites. She remembered seeing photos of what a black mamba could do to a person.

Pain. Convulsions. Paralysis. And there were even more drastic symptoms where people lost limbs. Where connective tissue broke down. Where the victim was unable to breathe.

"We've got to help him," she muttered, her palms suddenly sweaty.

"I know," Dillinger said. "But how are we going to do that without triggering that snake to strike Gabe?"

That was a good question.

What were they going to do?

CHAPTER TWENTY-EIGHT

GABE TRIED NOT TO MOVE. Tried not to breathe. Tried not to do anything to give the snake an indication he was a threat.

In other circumstances, Gabe would simply run from the snake. But the only way he could retreat right now was by opening the car door and darting out. In the time it took Gabe to do that, the snake could strike. Even with the medical clinic being right here, his survival would be iffy.

He had seen somebody in Africa one time who'd suffered a black mamba bite. The venom had spread through his entire body, and he'd died before medical help had arrived thirty minutes later.

As much faith as Gabe had in the medical staff

here at the clinic, he wasn't sure they were equipped to deal with something like this.

From his peripheral vision, he saw Autumn and Dillinger still standing there. He was grateful they had enough sense not to get any closer. Any movement could provoke the snake.

No doubt, the two of them were trying to figure out what to do. But Gabe didn't even know what to tell them. There was no good way out of the situation.

Whomever had left the snake in Gabe's vehicle had known that. They'd purposely put the snake there knowing this would be a no-win situation.

Sweat began to trickle down his temple.

He had to stay in control right now. Panicking would only get him killed.

As his mind raced through the possibilities of how he was going to get out of this, he came up empty. He had no idea what he was going to do. In all his training, he didn't ever remember going through the details of being stuck in a car with a venomous snake.

Gabe's reflexes might be fast, but he couldn't say with certainty they'd be faster than a snake's.

Lord, please help me now. Help Autumn and

Dillinger figure out what to do. Because one wrong move, and I could die.

Gabe wasn't ready to die yet. He hadn't even gotten up the nerve to tell Autumn how he felt.

How could someone so brave in some areas feel like such a coward when it came to his dream woman?

He needed to change that.

But first he had to get out of this alive.

"I NEED TO CALL ANIMAL CONTROL," Dillinger murmured as he stared at Gabe's car. "I want to help. But if we try to open this door . . ."

"Gabe will die." Autumn's throat tightened as she said the words. "We don't have time to wait for animal control to arrive. Basically, if we open that door, the motion could trigger the snake to strike."

"That's what I think also."

Autumn frowned as her mind raced. "We need to figure out something else that we can do right now."

"Any ideas?" Dillinger didn't move as he asked the question. Both of them knew each of their actions needed to be measured and purposeful.

Finding a solution had been all Autumn had

been able to think about. If Gabe wasn't trapped in a car, she'd have more ideas—nets or boxes or things of that sort. But the snake's close proximity to Gabe complicated all those ideas.

Think, Autumn. Think. There had to be *something* they could do.

At once, an idea hit her.

She didn't know if her plan would work. But the idea was worth looking into.

She pulled out her phone to do some quick research.

"What are you doing?" Dillinger peered over her shoulder.

"Give me a minute. I have an idea. I just need to double-check something first."

A few minutes later, she had the confirmation she needed and turned to Dillinger. "You stay here with Gabe just in case something happens. I need to run back in the clinic and get something."

"I shouldn't leave you . . ." He reluctantly shook his head.

"I'll be okay," she insisted.

In any other circumstance, Autumn might feel a rush of fear. But not right now. Right now, all she could think about was helping Gabe.

She darted into the clinic and found the supply

closet where they kept all the gas cannisters. It took a few minutes to find what she needed. She'd need to answer for her use of medical supplies later. But whatever the consequences might be, they would be worth it if her idea saved Gabe.

A few minutes later, she ran outside with a tank of nitrous oxide and a tube.

"What . . . ?" Dillinger squinted as he stared at her, not bothering to hide his confusion.

"Nitrous oxide has been proven to make snakes pass out," she explained as she tried to catch her breath. "It's used on pythons in some circumstances. It should work on this snake also."

Dillinger narrowed his eyes. "What about Gabe? Will it make him pass out also?"

"He's bigger, so he'll need to be exposed to a large amount of gas before he passes out. I need the snake to go to sleep first, and, once it does, we can grab Gabe before the gas affects him. Besides, I'll use a controlled amount and, even if it does knock him out, it will only be briefly. This won't harm the snake or Gabe. It will just sedate them until we can figure the situation out."

"If you say so," Dillinger said. "I called Cassidy and animal control. They're on their way. I ran into

Doc Clemson and told him what was happening, just in case we need him."

Autumn grasped the tube in her hands and began to connect it with the cannister of gas.

"How do you plan on running that inside without causing the snake to strike?" Dillinger asked.

"The moonroof is cracked open, just slightly," she said. "It's the most noninvasive way to go about it, and hopefully we can do it quietly so we don't elicit any reactions. What do you think?"

"I think it's worth a shot. From everything that I know about cars, that should work."

"Then let's do this. We don't have any time to waste."

CHAPTER TWENTY-NINE

GABE REMAINED FROZEN. But he was keenly aware that Autumn and Dillinger were doing something outside the car. He appreciated their subtle movements and low tones.

But he desperately wanted to know what they were up to.

He could trust Autumn, he reminded himself. She was brilliant and down to earth. Whatever she was doing, she would have thought it through. And Dillinger was also a former SEAL.

Though that brought him a measure of comfort, tension still threaded through him.

He wanted to glance at the snake again. To see what was happening.

Through his peripheral vision, he knew the

snake's head was raised. The creature clearly felt endangered, which was why it remained coiled with his head flattened. He thought he could see slowly, controlled tongue flicks. He heard the beast hissing.

The snake was definitely agitated. Definitely aggressive. Definitely deadly.

His heart continued to thump in his chest at a maddening rhythm.

He couldn't imagine what Autumn and Dillinger were planning right now. But he could very clearly hear them moving at the back of the car.

Then everything went silent.

Autumn and Dillinger stood a safe distance away from the car. At least, that's where Gabe thought they were.

He still refused to move. He couldn't move, not even a half inch.

More sweat trickled down his back.

If whatever they were planning didn't work, he was going to need a backup plan. The only thing he could think about doing was opening the car door, diving out, and praying the snake didn't catch him in time. Or if the creature did catch him that doctors would be able to prevent the spread of venom in his body.

His eyelids drooped.

His eyelids drooped? With all the adrenaline pumping through him, why was he feeling sleepy right now?

His head began to swirl.

What was going on?

He felt himself begin to lean forward but caught himself.

His heart pounded harder.

No movement, he told himself. No movement.

Movement would mean death.

But as Gabe felt himself start to lean again, he feared that it was too late.

"THE SNAKE LOOKS like it's relaxing," Autumn murmured as she stared through the windshield. "His head is sinking lower."

"Is it completely out?" Dillinger asked.

She nibbled on her bottom lip as she stared through the window. "I can't tell. But I hope so. Gabe is starting to nod off a little bit also."

She prayed her plan didn't backfire. There was so much that could go wrong.

"We have to act now," Dillinger murmured.

"You're right. I'll stay on the passenger side

where the snake is, and I'll open the door to distract it—just in case the gas isn't working. When I do that, you grab Gabe."

Dillinger stared at her. "Are you sure you want to do that? If that snake isn't out . . ."

Her lungs tightened, but she nodded anyway. "I'll be fine. Besides, I won't be able to pull Gabe out like you can. I'm not strong enough."

His jaw tightened, but he nodded. "Okay then. Let's do this. Now."

Autumn moved to one door and Dillinger to the other. They exchanged a nod, and Autumn gently pulled the door handle.

Her gaze remained on the snake.

But it didn't move.

Maybe that gas had done the trick.

As she did that, Dillinger threw the driver's door open. In a fluid movement, he grabbed Gabe and jerked him from the front seat then shut the door.

The gas hadn't totally taken effect on Gabe yet. He managed to find his footing and stumble away from the vehicle. Dillinger kept an arm around him until he got his bearings.

As they scrambled away, Autumn slammed her door closed, making sure the snake stayed in the vehicle.

With Gabe safe, she turned the gas off and rushed toward him. Dillinger kept his arm around Gabe as they retreated toward the clinic.

Once they reached the entrance, Dillinger lowered Gabe onto a bench to get some fresh air. The effects of the gas faded quickly now that he wasn't breathing it in. Doc Clemson and Nurse Hannah also joined them.

Autumn pulled out a penlight to check his eyes. His pupils appeared fine.

"Gabe?" Her heart pounded in her ears as she waited for him to respond.

He blinked several times, still looking dazed. Finally, he seemed to snap out of it and ran a hand through his hair. He sucked in several deep breaths before turning to them.

"What happened?" he muttered.

Autumn and Dillinger exchanged a glance, unspoken relief stretching between them.

Gabe was okay. He was really okay.

Praise God.

Autumn kept a hand on his shoulder. "You gave us quite a scare back there."

"I don't know what you guys did but thank you."

Autumn nodded, wishing all her worry had

subsided. But it hadn't. Not yet. "Maybe we should get you inside as you recover."

As soon as she said the words, Cassidy pulled into the lot, animal control behind her.

The police chief and her team were going to need to handle the snake situation themselves. Right now, Autumn wanted to focus her full attention on making sure Gabe was okay.

CHAPTER THIRTY

"ANIMAL CONTROL REMOVED THE SNAKE," Cassidy told Gabe as the three of them sat in Autumn's office an hour later. "It was a black mamba."

Autumn shivered upon hearing the confirmation. She didn't know much about snakes, but she knew that type wasn't one to be messed with.

Gabe took another sip of water as he leaned back in his chair. "It's native to Africa and extremely venomous. It's also one of the fastest moving snakes in the world, and its venom can kill someone in twenty minutes."

Autumn felt her skin grow paler. "How did someone even get the snake to Lantern Beach? Into the US? Are they legal?"

"We'll be looking into that, as well as trying to figure out exactly what to do with the snake." Cassidy turned to Autumn, a touch of admiration in her gaze. "That was some pretty quick thinking you did back there. I'm impressed."

Cassidy's team was still processing the scene. From what Gabe had heard, Autumn had run some kind of gas into the vehicle to knock the snake out. Who would have ever thought of a plan like that?

Gabe knew.

Autumn would.

His respect for the woman only grew.

"There's some security footage in the parking lot," Cassidy said. "We're going to try to figure out exactly who left that for you. How many people knew about those black mambas from Africa?"

Gabe shrugged. "It's hard to say. Clearly, the guys on our team did. I'm sure we told our superiors as well. But we never mentioned the snakes in any articles or interviews if that's what you're talking about."

"I see," Cassidy said.

Gabe shifted in his seat as he continued to process the situation. "So you're thinking that whoever is behind this is close enough to us that they would know that kind of information?"

Cassidy grimaced. "It's the only thing that makes sense to me."

"I have to hand it to whoever is behind this . . . not only are they deadly but they're creative." Gabe shook his head, realizing how these people were wasting their abilities on harming others when they could be put to good use.

"You can say that again," Cassidy said. "I'm going to check out the security footage now. But if there's anything else you need . . ."

Gabe nodded. "And if you need anything from me, please let me know."

As she closed the door behind her, Gabe and Autumn were finally alone.

They glanced at each other.

How did Gabe even tell Autumn thank you for all she'd done?

And how exactly did these crimes that were occurring against both of them tie together?

They had to be getting closer to finding answers. But the closer they got to those answers, the more determined somebody else became to kill them.

Gabe's heart pounded into his ears at the thought.

AUTUMN FELT her throat go dry as she stared across her desk at Gabe. There was so much she wanted to say to him. So many feelings simmering beneath the surface.

She'd been wrong about him. When she'd first seen him from a distance, she'd assumed he was immature and impulsive. But now she realized that he was one of the bravest people she'd ever met.

When she'd thought that she might lose him, unexpected feelings had risen to the surface. Feelings she wanted to pretend weren't there. Feelings she never wanted to feel again, not after Stanley. She'd been too afraid of having her heart broken again.

As she remembered what Gabe had shared with her about his childhood, it only made her respect for him grow even more. He'd risen above hard circumstances and had made something of himself.

Yet he had no one there to be proud of him. No one to be there at all.

It wasn't right. Everyone deserved to have somebody behind them cheering them on or picking them up when they fell.

She stood to refill his water. But as she handed him the cup, he rose also.

The same tension she felt also stretched across his gaze.

"I just want to thank you again for everything you've done." Gabe's voice sounded low and husky with emotion. "If you hadn't acted as quickly as you did, this might be a totally different situation right now."

Autumn swallowed hard as she felt emotions welling in her, nearly clogging her throat. "I'm glad it all worked out. I was nervous there for a while, but somehow it all came together."

"It worked out because you're a brilliant woman, Autumn Spenser." Admiration rang through his voice, and the smoky look remained in his eyes.

Her pulse quickened as she felt the tension pulling between them. "I don't know about that. But I was praying hard, and I'm so glad the idea hit me."

He lowered his head and stepped closer. "Whoever is behind this isn't going to give up, you know?"

She nodded, worry gripping her and tightening her lungs until it felt impossible to get a deep breath. "I know. There's really no end in sight for this, is there?"

"I want you to know that I'm not going to let anything happen to you." His voice sounded low and husky—and full of sincere promise.

She stepped closer and glanced up into his warm gaze. "You do know that's a promise impossible to keep."

"Why do you say that?" Gabe's gaze probed into hers.

"Because you're an incredibly brave and strong man. But these guys are determined. And if something does happen to me—"

"I mean it, Autumn. I'm not going to let that happen."

"Gabe . . ." Autumn licked her lips, trying to find the words to say. How did she let Gabe know that it was okay and that it wasn't his fault if something happened to her?

"Yes?" He waited for her response.

"You don't have to prove yourself to me." She reached up on her tiptoes and planted a kiss on his cheek.

As she lowered herself back down on her feet, she saw his pupils widen. Heard his breath catch. Saw his body go rigid.

Maybe she shouldn't have done that.

Yet another part of her didn't regret it—even if it did mean she couldn't be his doctor anymore.

CHAPTER THIRTY-ONE

GABE STARED AT AUTUMN, his cheek burning as if he'd touched fire.

As his gaze caught with Autumn's, his thoughts rushed.

Was it possible that Autumn might return his feelings? Or had that kiss on the cheek simply been a friendly gesture? A way of saying thanks?

"Autumn . . ." His voice came out scratchier than he'd wanted.

She said nothing, only stared back with her eyes wide and curious.

Gabe stepped closer, and his hands went to her waist. He leaned forward and his lips met hers. He hesitated, giving her a chance to back away.

But she didn't.

His hands move from her waist to her neck. As he pulled her closer, his fingers tangled in her hair. Their lips continued to explore each other's.

When they finally pulled away, Gabe felt breathless as he stared at her. His heartbeat pounded in his ears, and his head felt like it was swirling.

He never thought a woman could have this kind of effect on him. But he felt like putty in Autumn's hands.

"I was wondering when you were going to do that," Autumn murmured.

A grin spread across his face. "Were you?"

She rested her hand on his chest. "I was actually hoping that it might have happened a little sooner. But I'm not complaining."

Warmth bubbled inside him. Gabe reached up and pushed the hair out of her face, out of her eyes.

She was so beautiful. So smart. Entirely too good for him.

It almost felt surreal that any of this was happening.

You don't have to prove yourself to me.

Her words echoed in his head. Something about them seemed to release him from the years of pressure he'd felt after hearing his father say that he'd never amount to anything. Wasn't that exactly what

Gabe had been trying to do since then? To prove to himself that his father was wrong?

But something about hearing Autumn's words made him feel like he didn't have to try to do that anymore, made him feel a sense of relief that he didn't know was even possible.

"I'm so glad you're okay." Autumn's voice cracked as she said the words. "When I saw you in that car with the snake . . ."

She didn't finish the statement. Instead, her eyes misted as she rubbed her throat as if fighting tears.

"I know," he said quietly. "I know."

She threw her arms around him, and he leaned into her, relishing the sweet scent of wildflowers that filled his nostrils. If he had his way, he'd never let go. He knew that wasn't possible right now.

But suddenly, his future looked a little brighter.

As much as he wished that this was it and the two of them could live happily ever after, Gabe knew there were other issues at hand.

Issues like keeping Autumn and himself alive.

AUTUMN STILL COULDN'T BELIEVE what had just happened, nor could she believe how incredible

Gabe's lips had felt against hers. She never wanted the moment to end.

But reality couldn't be ignored.

Gabe's thoughts seemed to mirror hers. He stepped back, still grasping one of her hands with his own until reluctantly letting go.

"Whatever is in the paperwork Dr. Johnson sent you . . . someone wants it." His gaze looked stormy, and his taut muscles showed he was clearly upset.

Gabe's words made sense. That paperwork *had* put her in danger, hadn't it?

She pushed down the rush of panic she felt. "So what do we do? Do you want me to hole up here at the clinic?"

"It's not secure here. I'd like to take you back to the Blackout headquarters. We have extra apartments there where you can stay if you're comfortable with that."

The idea of being at a secure location did bring her a measure of comfort. Especially if Gabe was nearby too. "I can do that. At least until this passes."

"The other issue comes with getting you there." Gabe frowned as if already trying to figure out the logistics of that.

"What are you thinking?"

"My gut tells me that whoever is behind this is

watching us and waiting for you to leave. Travel is going to be when you're the most vulnerable. My gut is telling me that these guys are going to strike again."

She shivered. "You really think so?"

"I do. But I have a plan."

Her curiosity spiked. "What's up?"

"Let me make a few calls, and then I'll run it past you."

Autumn couldn't wait to hear what his plan was. But on the other hand, the thought of what they were having to go through to keep her safe caused a shot of terror to fill her.

Much like a fever, this was only going to get worse before it got better.

CHAPTER THIRTY-TWO

THIRTY MINUTES LATER, CJ Compton arrived at the clinic. She also worked for Blackout. The woman was petite and muscular and didn't overall resemble Autumn. But Gabe hoped this plan would work.

Autumn stared at Gabe when she saw CJ, still appearing confused. "I don't understand."

CJ quickly introduced herself before reaching into a bag. She pulled on a reddish-brown wig, one similar in style and color to Autumn's hair.

"CJ is going to pretend to be you and leave with me to take you back to Blackout," Gabe explained. "In the meantime, you're going ride in an ambulance dressed as a paramedic. One of my guys will be with you and take you to the Blackout headquarters."

Autumn's eyes widened. "That seems like a lot of trouble to go through for me . . ."

"You're worth it." Gabe pulled her closer and lowered his voice. "I meant what I said earlier. We have to take every precaution necessary. Your life depends on it."

She rubbed her arms and shivered.

He hadn't wanted to be so blunt, but he had no choice if he wanted to drive home his point.

"Okay," she finally said. "We can do that."

"I'm going to need your lab coat," CJ called from the corner where she began to transform into Autumn.

"Of course." Autumn pulled it off and handed it to her.

"And we're going to need an extra paramedic uniform for you," Gabe told her.

"I know where I can get one of those," Autumn said.

Gabe hoped they could pull this off.

It was the best plan they had right now but still riskier than he'd like.

AUTUMN COULDN'T REMEMBER the last time she had felt this anxious.

Could they really pull off this ruse? It seemed risky. But maybe their plan to trick their pursuers was possible.

She glanced in a mirror behind her office door. She'd donned the paramedic's uniform. Her red hair was tucked up into a baseball cap. Reading glasses rested on the bridge of her nose. From a distance, she might not be recognizable.

Beckett had also donned a paramedic's uniform. He would go with her in the ambulance.

And so much could go wrong.

She rubbed her temples, trying not to worry too much.

Gabe stepped closer and rubbed her arms before murmuring, "It's going to be okay."

He sounded convincing, and Autumn hoped his words were true.

She turned toward him, wishing she could freeze this moment and stay here in her office, safe with Gabe. But that wasn't a possibility. "I'll feel better once I'm at the Blackout headquarters."

"That's understandable. You put Dr. Johnson's notes somewhere safe?"

"I made a copy of them to bring with me. Then I

hid the originals in the room where we keep all the controlled substances here at the clinic. It's the most secure area I could think of. I also took photos of every page, just in case. I couldn't risk losing the information. Plus, this way I can review the notes while I'm at Blackout, or wherever I am for that matter."

"Smart thinking." Gabe nodded at the door. "I've got to go meet CJ. As soon as we've left in the car, Beckett will come to you, and you can ride in the ambulance. Do you understand?"

Autumn nodded. But she really wished Gabe would be with her.

He stepped closer and planted a soft kiss on her forehead. "I'll see you at the Blackout headquarters, okay?"

"Okay . . ."

Gabe took a step back.

"Wait . . ."

He paused, his blue eyes widening with inquiry. "Yes?"

"What if something happens to you?" Her voice cracked.

All she'd been able to think about was that possibility. A lot of these crimes seemed to be centered on her. What if Gabe was a casualty, and it was her fault?

"I'll be okay," he assured her.

Autumn stared up at him another moment longer and saw a mix of strength and compassion hovering in his gaze. She wouldn't change his mind on this. Gabe was going to go through with his plan whether she liked it or not.

"Be careful." Her voice felt raw as the words left her lips. "And when you get back to the Blackout headquarters, I want that hot fudge sundae we never got last time."

A wide smile slowly spread across his face. "It's a deal."

CHAPTER THIRTY-THREE

GABE PUT his hand on CJ's back as he led her outside. It wasn't something he'd normally do, but he had to act like CJ was actually Autumn.

He glanced around the parking lot, but no one suspicious caught his eye. Then again, no one suspicious had ever caught his eye—not since this started. These guys were top-notch at what they were doing.

Rocco and Axel had driven to a side road and parked out of sight there. If anyone followed either Autumn or Gabe, those two would pull out and act as backup.

As he spotted Autumn's car in the distance, Gabe's throat went dry as he remembered finding that snake earlier. He knew the police were investigating it. They'd taken any prints from his door and inside his car. They were researching also where the snake had come from. He could only hope they got some answers.

He also knew Autumn's car had been thoroughly checked by the police earlier as a precaution. So when he and CJ climbed in, there shouldn't be any surprises waiting for them.

That didn't help his lungs loosen, however. All he could think about was that snake and how close to death that he had come.

Gabe took the keys from CJ, just as if Autumn might be handing them to him right now. He helped CJ into the car before climbing behind the wheel.

He released a breath as he started the engine. "Here goes nothing."

"Here goes nothing," CJ echoed.

He backed from the space and started down the road. The drive to the Blackout headquarters was only about ten minutes. Darkness hung around them, which could be their friend or enemy, depending on how it all worked out.

He scanned everything around him for any sign of trouble.

As he did, he spotted the ambulance's flashing lights behind him.

Autumn.

This was all a part of their plan.

Gabe pulled to the side of the road and waited for the vehicle to speed past before he pulled back onto the road and followed.

Autumn should be in the ambulance right now. She would get to the Blackout headquarters before he did.

That fact brought him a small measure of comfort. The last thing he needed was for this road to be blockaded in some type of standoff with Autumn waiting in the ambulance behind the whole scene. No, it was much better this way.

When it disappeared from sight, he let out a breath as relief filled him.

But his reprieve was short-lived.

Headlights suddenly appeared behind him.

Instinctively, he knew that this was the driver who'd nearly killed him.

AUTUMN GLANCED out the back window of the ambulance, trying to see what was going on.

So far, Gabe appeared safe.

Maybe this *would* work.

She prayed that was the case.

Beckett glanced over at her. "We're not that far away from the campus."

She nodded, knowing that should make her feel better. But until Gabe got back also, it wouldn't.

She continued to stare at the road behind them, waiting for something bad to happen.

As she did, a car appeared behind Gabe.

Her pulse quickened.

"Beckett . . ." Her voice cracked as she said his name.

He followed her gaze and frowned. "Don't get upset yet. This is what we expected would happen."

"What now?" Her voice continued to tremble as she asked the question.

"We're going to keep an eye on them." Beckett sounded calm and in control, like this was routine. "Rocco and Axel should be behind them. Whoever is pursuing us will be trapped between the two cars."

She wished that made her feel better. "But these guys always have tricks up their sleeve. It's not like they're just going to surrender."

"My team contains some of the best operatives there are. Even Junior."

She glanced at Beckett. "Junior, huh?"

He smiled. "I think of Gabe as a little brother.

He's a good guy—a good guy that I like to give a hard time."

She nodded and touched her throat, continuing to pray that everything would work out.

But as she watched, an explosion filled the air on the road behind them.

A scream lodged in her throat.

CHAPTER THIRTY-FOUR

GABE WATCHED as CJ threw a flash bang from the window. A moment later, an explosion sounded behind them. Smoke filled the air, and the driver pursuing them swerved. As they did, Rocco and Axel pulled up behind them.

Whoever was in that car was trapped.

Gabe and his team had whoever was in that vehicle just where they wanted them.

Gabe pressed on the brakes and threw the car in Park. Moving quickly, he withdrew his gun and climbed out. CJ did the same.

They hurried through the smoky remains of the flash bang. Rocco and Axel were already there with their guns drawn and pointed at the car.

The person driving that vehicle would have no choice but to surrender.

"Come out with your hands up," Rocco called. "You're not walking away from this."

Gabe waited, trying to see through the haze. Would the driver be someone he recognized?

He didn't think so.

But he didn't know what to think at this point either.

Gabe held his breath, still waiting.

Finally, the door opened, and a man stepped out with his hands up.

When Gabe saw the face, he balked.

"Max Anderson?"

What was one of his former colleagues doing behind that wheel?

AUTUMN FELT beside herself as the ambulance pulled into the Blackout headquarters.

She had no idea what was happening on the road right now. She could only guess.

But everything she imagined wasn't good. Everything she imagined ended in fatalities. That wasn't the image that she wanted in her head.

The ambulance parked and Beckett ushered her into the main building, almost as if he feared there could be danger out here.

As soon as they stepped inside, his phone rang. He muttered a few indiscernible things into the device before ending the call and turning toward her.

"Everyone's okay," he assured her. "Gabe wanted me to let you know that. He said you should just keep studying Dr. Johnson's papers until the rest of the team is able to get back."

She nodded quickly as relief filled her.

That made sense. The sooner she could figure out what was on these pages that was worth killing for, the sooner the Blackout guys would know how to proceed.

But it was going to be hard to concentrate with her being safe inside and Gabe being out in the middle of danger.

If she and Gabe pursued a relationship . . . if that's what they decided they were going to do . . . then this would be her future.

Could she live like this?

She'd like to say yes.

But the worried feeling rumbling in her stomach

was something she never wanted to experience again.

She'd be wise to keep that in mind.

CHAPTER THIRTY-FIVE

GABE WATCHED as Max scowled and put his gun on the ground just as he'd been instructed. Nobody else was in the car, just Max.

"What are you doing here?" Rocco demanded. As a senior member of the team, he'd taken charge.

"I don't know what you're talking about." Defiance flickered in Max's gaze.

Max had always been a bit of an outcast, the one in the group who hadn't bonded with the rest of the team. Gabe had actually been relieved whenever he went on a mission and didn't have to work with Max. He was one of those guys Gabe had never been sure they could trust.

It looked like he'd been right.

"Don't play stupid with us." Rocco scowled and stepped closer. "You're involved with this. Why?"

Max's jaw remained stiff. "I don't know what you're talking about. I heard you guys were here, and I was taking a drive to see if maybe we could catch up."

His words lacked sincerity. Instead, he sounded like he was playing some kind of twisted game.

"We all know that explanation doesn't make sense," Rocco said. "We were never that close. You're going to need to do better than that."

"I'm afraid I can't do any better." Max's voice nearly sounded monotone and apathetic. "I was just taking a drive. There's nothing illegal about that. In fact, I'm the one who should be reporting you guys. You nearly caused me to get into an accident when you threw out that flash bang."

"No one is buying what you're trying to sell." Rocco shook his head, his jaw hard. "So we can do this the easy way or the hard way."

"Then I guess it's going to be the hard way." Max raised his chin in noncooperation. "I'm not admitting to anything."

Anger burned through Gabe's blood. He started to step closer when Axel grabbed his arm and pulled him back.

Gabe knew there was a right and a wrong way to do things. Right now, the right way to deal with Max would be to call the police.

But before they could, sirens sounded in the background.

The police were already on their way.

Maybe Cassidy and her team could get something out of this guy. But one thing Max had said was correct. They had no proof he'd done anything wrong. Would the police even be able to hold him?

They were about to find out.

Gabe prayed they hadn't come this far to hit another roadblock.

AS AUTUMN POURED over Dr. Johnson's notes, her cell phone buzzed.

She looked away from the research and ran her hand over her eyes, feeling more exhausted than she should. Maybe a message would be a nice break from everything she'd been studying.

But as she glanced at the phone screen, a number she hadn't seen in a long time popped up there.

Stanley Jackson's.

Her ex-fiancé.

She bit the inside of her lip, wondering why he would be contacting her. After a moment of hesitation, she lifted the phone.

A text message stretched across the screen there.

HEY, **Autumn. It's Stanley. I'm staying here on Lantern Beach, and I'm hoping to talk to you. What do you think?**

HER EYEBROWS SHOT UP. Why would Stanley be here in Lantern Beach? What sense did that make? Even more so—what could he possibly want to talk to her about?

The questions collided in her head.

She stared at her phone another moment, trying to figure out how to respond.

Then another thought slammed into her mind.

Could Stanley be on the island because he had something to do with what was going on?

Her heart pounded into her chest at the thought.

She didn't want to believe it. But she didn't want to be naive either.

"Any luck?" a deep voice filled the room.

She nearly dropped her phone.

Relief filled her when she saw Gabe standing in the doorway. She rushed from her chair and strode toward him.

He was here. More importantly, he was okay.

She pulled him into a hug. "I'm so glad to see you."

He held her close before murmuring, "I'm doing just fine."

Autumn decided to ignore Stanley's text for now, and, instead, she lowered herself back into the chair. Gabe pulled a seat in front of her and sat there, their knees touching.

"What happened?" She was anxious to hear if their plan had worked.

But if it had worked, why did Gabe look so unhappy right now?

"We were able to catch the guy," he started. "It turns out, he's somebody the guys and I worked with in the military."

She gasped at his revelation. "What?"

Gabe nodded, a new hardness in his gaze. "We can't believe it either."

"Did he say what he's doing here?"

"He's not giving us any details, unfortunately."

She frowned as she let that information sink in.

"That just makes all of this even more confusing, doesn't it?"

"It does. We had no choice but to turn him over to Cassidy. We're hoping she'll get some information from him about what's going on."

"We can only hope." She crossed her arms and leaned back.

"How's your research going?"

She glanced at the papers scattered across the table. "I'm still looking at his notes and trying to make sense of everything. But it looks like Dr. Johnson discovered some type of new chemical protocol and began researching it."

"Do you think that chemical protocol had something to do with what was sprayed on us in Africa?"

She frowned. "I'm not sure yet. It's a lot of information to look through. But that's my best guess at this point."

Gabe sighed and stared off into the distance. "How would Dr. Johnson have gotten hold of chemicals these terrorists were using over in Africa?"

Autumn shook her head. She'd asked herself that same question. "I have no idea."

"Hopefully, with some more time, you'll be able to find out those answers."

"I hope so." She frowned as she thought about

that text Stanley had sent her. Should she mention it to Gabe? She knew that she probably should. So why was she hesitating? It just seemed unimportant considering everything else that was going on.

"Autumn? What are you thinking?" Gabe narrowed his eyes as he studied her face.

She hesitated another moment before grabbing her phone and finding the text. Instead of reading it aloud, she showed Gabe her screen.

His eyes widened as he read the message.

"This is Stanley, your ex-fiancé?" he asked.

"Yes, the one who cheated on me. I haven't talk to him in at least a year. I have no idea why he's contacting me now or why he just happens to be here in Lantern Beach."

Gabe's jaw tightened. "Maybe it's because he's involved in this."

"I thought about that too. I find it hard to believe that he would be. Then again, I don't know what to think anymore." She glanced at her phone again. "I don't know how to respond."

Gabe rubbed his shoulder again, as if it had begun to ache. "Let me talk to the rest of the team. If this guy is somehow involved, maybe we can make him talk. What did you say that he does for a living?"

Autumn felt her throat go dry. Why hadn't she

thought about this before? Maybe it was the connection they'd been looking for.

She licked her lips. "Stanley is a government contractor . . . and he sells supplies to the military."

"Supplies?"

"Medical supplies."

CHAPTER THIRTY-SIX

"WE DEFINITELY NEED to talk to Stanley," Colton said. "He could very well be the link we're looking for here."

The team, along with Autumn, had gathered in the conference room and were discussing their options on how to proceed.

They'd also talked about Max.

The man still hadn't opened up, despite Cassidy's interrogation. In fact, he'd called in a lawyer, which was never a good sign.

There was too much on the line to mess this up.

"If Autumn is supposed to be meeting Stanley, but then we show up . . . how do you think that's going to go over?" Gabe asked.

"As soon as he sees you, he won't talk," Autumn said. "Just like Max."

Gabe turned to her, curious about the new tone to her voice. "Then what do you suggest?"

Determination filled her gaze. "Let me go."

Gabe shook his head, the reaction instantaneous. "That sounds like a terrible idea."

"But she might be right," Colton said. "She's the most likely one to get Stanley talking."

"She's also the most likely one to get killed." Gabe crossed his arms, not backing down.

"I don't think Stanley would hurt me like that," Autumn said. "Break my heart? Sure. But I can't see him physically harming me."

"Desperate people do desperate things," Gabe said. "I've seen it one too many times. If Stanley is involved in this, then he might be desperate to keep you quiet."

Autumn lowered her head and ran a hand through her hair. "You're probably right. I can't deny that, nor can I claim to have more experience than you guys with these types of things. All I know is that if we want answers, I need to go myself . . . alone."

Gabe felt his throat tighten as her final word

echoed in his head. *Alone.* "What if things go wrong?"

"What if we meet somewhere public?" Autumn said. "What if you guys are close? What if I'm wired?"

"Things could still go wrong." Gabe frowned, still not liking the idea of this.

"Things can always go wrong," she reminded him. "Always. On the field. On the operating table. Life isn't without risk. I'm going to have to take some of those risks also."

Gabe's jaw tightened. He didn't like the sound of this—not in the least. But he also knew Autumn was right. They were going to have to make some hard choices here.

"If you're sure you're okay with it, Autumn, I think we should proceed," Colton said. "The people behind this are escalating, and we need to put an end to it."

Gabe didn't say anything, even though he knew that his friend's words were true.

Colton's gaze traveled to meet everyone's in the room. No one argued.

Finally, Colton nodded. "It sounds like we have a plan. Now, let's get these details worked out so we can make sure that nothing goes wrong. Autumn, we need you to text Stanley back and tell him that you can meet. Then we'll let you know all the details. Are you sure you're okay with this?"

Autumn didn't hesitate before announcing, "I am."

Gabe wished he felt that certain.

AUTUMN FELT her nerves bubbling inside her as she studied herself in the mirror, but she pushed her anxiety down. She had to think positive thoughts to get through this.

She'd meet Stanley, find out what he had to say, and then get this over with.

You can do this, Autumn. No worries.

She'd agreed to meet Stanley in public—at a bench on the boardwalk. Blackout agents would be lingering close and listening. They'd even wired her so they could hear everything being said. At the first sign of trouble, they'd step in.

Even though Autumn knew she was in good hands, that didn't change the fact that something could easily go wrong.

She adjusted her outfit one more time. She'd

changed and borrowed some clothes so she could conceal the wire beneath her blouse.

Just as she glanced in the mirror one last time, a knock sounded at the door of her temporary apartment. She strode toward it, knowing someone was coming to fetch her because it was time to go.

Gabe stood there, that same worried look on his face that he'd worn earlier when they'd come up with this plan.

He stepped inside and shut the door behind him before pausing in front of her. "You sure you want to do this?"

She nodded, even though her neck and shoulders felt stiff. "I'm sure. But thank you for looking out for me."

Gabe pushed a lock of her hair behind her ear, his gaze warm with concern. "I don't want anything to happen to you."

She rested her palm on the side of his face, studying the slight bruise from his accident. The cut near his jaw. Feeling a slight scruff beneath her skin. The action felt natural, like she'd done it a million times before.

"I know," she said quietly. "I know."

He wrapped his arms around her shoulders, pulling her close until she nestled beneath his chin.

"All you have to do is say the magic word, and I'll be there."

The magic word? *Doritos*.

It had been Gabe's idea.

"Got it." She smiled but the action quickly faded as the reality of the situation hit her again. "Still nothing on Max?"

He shook his head. "I don't think he's going to be talking. I did make a few phone calls, and it appears he took a job with the Dagger Group."

She pulled back so she could see Gabe's face. "What does that mean? What's the Dagger Group?"

"It's another private security firm. I think someone hired Max and a couple other people to do their dirty work here on Lantern Beach." He paused. "Does Stanley have money?"

Autumn thought about it before nodding. "Most people would consider him well-off, I suppose. He could probably afford to hire someone."

"That's what I'm afraid of."

"But it doesn't make sense. I don't know why Stanley would be involved in something like this, even if he does sell supplies to the military . . ."

Gabe frowned, his soft gaze reassuring her. "I'm not saying that he's involved in this, but we need to make sure that he's not."

"I understand." Autumn leaned back and straightened her shoulders. "I guess we better get going before I'm late."

Gabe nodded, but familiar worry filled his gaze.

He placed a hand on her back as he led her through the building. She'd drive herself to the boardwalk with Gabe in the vehicle. He'd stay low in case anyone saw them. The rest of the Blackout team would tail her in a different car.

Autumn knew they were worried she'd encounter trouble on the drive there, and she appreciated their concern. If she were honest with herself, she was concerned also.

But she could do this. She had no choice except to try.

Because sometimes life required brave things.

That was what it was requiring of her now.

CHAPTER THIRTY-SEVEN

GABE SAT on a nearby bench with an open news-
paper in front of him and sunglasses on his face.
From here, he had the perfect vantage point to watch
Autumn as she waited for Stanley.

The thought of her talking to her ex sent a surge
of jealousy through him.

Maybe *jealousy* wasn't the right word.

Stanley clearly hadn't known what a treasure he
had when he'd been engaged to Autumn. Still, the
idea of Autumn seeing her ex-fiancé now, right as
something between Gabe and Autumn might be
getting off the ground, did something strange to his
heart.

More than that, Gabe was worried this guy might
be behind the threats against Autumn. Beckett had

stayed back at headquarters to dig into Stanley's background. Gabe was interested to see what he turned up.

Gabe's gaze went to the boardwalk.

The area was swarming with tourists today, all trying to get in their last-minute vacations for the summer. Everyone looked so happy as they strolled with popcorn and ice cream in their hands and sunburns on their noses.

A moment of envy shot through Gabe. This was the exact kind of thing he'd wanted when growing up—happy memories of family vacations. But that hadn't worked out for him. He hoped, however, that one day he *could* make those kind of memories with a family of his own.

With Autumn?

His heart pounded harder.

It was too early to say. But there was something about the idea that he liked.

A man walking down the boardwalk caught Gabe's eye. He fit the description of Stanley. Could it be him?

Gabe glanced back at Autumn and saw that she'd straightened.

She recognized the man. It *had* to be Stanley.

Gabe glanced at the man again, looking for any

signs he had a weapon on him. But Gabe saw nothing.

The man looked exactly how Gabe thought he might. He had blond hair cut tight on the sides and high on the top. It was styled with a thick gel and had been brushed back in an oversize poof at the top of his head that looked immune to the area's humidity. His clothes looked designer and expensive. His tan didn't quite look natural. He had the gait of a salesman—full of confidence and charm.

Gabe already didn't like him.

He looked back at Autumn again and saw her hands clutched together in front of her. She wasn't happy to see Stanley either. In fact, she looked nervous.

If Gabe could talk to her now, he'd tell her to soften her shoulders. To relax her gaze. To loosen her jaw. But she was a smart woman and would figure this out on her own.

"Stanley," Autumn's voice rang through his earbuds. She sounded stiff and not thrilled, to say the least. To sound any other way wouldn't be believable.

"Autumn . . . don't you look beautiful? Beach life really suits you."

Gabe blanched as he watched Stanley lean

forward and plant a soft kiss on her cheek. Autumn remained stiff as if she didn't welcome the greeting. Instead, she nodded to the bench and Stanley lowered himself there.

Gabe continued to grip the newspaper, trying not to be too obvious that he was watching them. But his eyes were glued to the scene.

"I can't believe you're here," Autumn said.

"I wanted to see you."

"So you came here just to see me? I wasn't aware you even knew I'd come to Lantern Beach."

"It wasn't hard to find out. I just had to ask around to a few people."

"I see." Autumn's voice made it clear that she didn't appreciate the inquiries.

Gabe drew his gaze away from them as he saw someone else walking down the boardwalk. Unlike most of the people milling about this area, there was no family with this guy. He was by himself and walking as if on a mission.

Could this be another one of the guys involved with the Dagger Group? Probably more than one culprit was here on the island. Based on the way this guy carried himself, he had a military presence about him.

"Five o'clock, guys," Gabe muttered into his comm.

"I see him too," Rocco said. "I'll keep my eyes on him. I'm pretty sure he has a gun at his waist."

Gabe's muscles tightened even more.

He'd known this was a bad idea. On so many levels.

But now he had no choice but to wait until he had the signal to act.

AUTUMN FELT a rush of disgust rise in her. She couldn't believe that she was sitting here talking to Stanley. This man had a lot of nerve.

He looked the same as always—impeccably put together. Every hair was in place. Every tooth was shiny. Every word was measured and precise.

Every aspect of Stanley's life seemed to involve taking on a sales presentation persona, even when it had come to her. Their initial meeting had seemed like a coincidence at first. Autumn found out later it had been arranged.

Back in Baltimore, she'd gone to the same coffee shop every day. Stanley had seen her there and had pretended to accidentally spill his iced coffee on her, just so they'd have the chance to talk. The next day, when she'd shown up to place her order, Stanley was there. He'd already ordered her favorite drink for her as an apology.

But none of it had been real. Everything had all been a ruse to meet her, to get her to like him.

By the time Autumn had learned the truth, she was dating Stanley and she'd brushed it off as part of his charm. But, now, looking back, it just seemed like manipulation.

She forced herself not to avert her gaze and glance at the Blackout guys. She knew they were close and that they were watching, listening. If anything happened, they would move in. Besides, Autumn was out in public right now. She should be safe.

But that didn't stop the unease from jostling inside her.

She glanced back at Stanley and saw a thin layer of sweat on his forehead. "I'm still not sure why you're here."

"I was hoping we could catch up for a few minutes first, but if you want to jump right into it, I can do that too."

"Yes, please." Autumn pushed her sunglasses up higher, grateful for them, not only because the sun was bearing down on the bench, but also so Stanley couldn't see the thoughts running through her gaze.

She thought about how grateful she was she'd gotten out of this relationship before the two of them had tied the knot. Their breakup had felt devastating at the time, but now she could see it was a blessing in disguise.

Stanley shifted and ran his hands down his khaki shorts before turning toward her. Before he could speak, Autumn saw Rocco crossing the boardwalk.

Crossing the boardwalk? What was going on? Did he know something she didn't?

She'd turned off her earpiece so she couldn't hear anything they said. She didn't want to have the Blackout guys in her head as she was talking to Stanley. It was unnerving enough to know they were listening.

"I've been thinking about us, Autumn," Stanley started. "I realize that I made a huge mistake when I let you get away."

Her eyebrows shot up. *That* hadn't been what she had expected to hear. "What?"

She'd clearly heard him, but Autumn needed to buy some more time to process that information.

"It's true, Autumn. Robyn and I broke up. I

realize that what I had with you was a once in a lifetime thing."

She kept her face expressionless. "You came all the way here to tell me about that?"

"I wanted to talk face-to-face. I was hoping you'd see the sincerity in my eyes and hear it in my voice."

Instead of looking into his eyes, Autumn glanced at the Blackout guys again. Something was definitely going on. Otherwise, they wouldn't be moving like this.

Was it Stanley? Did they see something on him that she couldn't see? A gun?

She didn't think so. It would be visible with his outfit.

But something was definitely wrong.

"Autumn?" Stanley stared at her, confusion knotting his brow. "What do you think?"

She pulled her gaze from Gabe and glanced at Stanley. "What was that?"

"Did you hear a word I said?"

His condescending tone made her remember exactly why they hadn't been good together. "I'm sorry. I thought I saw somebody I knew. Could you say that again?"

She licked her lips and tried to focus on Stanley,

tried to trust that the Blackout guys would handle any situation that arose.

"Basically, what I said was this: I'd like for you to give me another chance, Autumn."

Autumn stared at Stanley, still trying to comprehend this conversation. "Are you saying that's the only reason you came here to Lantern Beach?"

A knot formed between his eyes as he shrugged. "Of course. Why else would I come here?"

"Vacation?"

He shrugged, looking annoyed as his shoulders and face tightened. "Autumn what's going on? Why are you acting so strangely?"

Her gaze trailed Rocco as he seemed to follow someone down the boardwalk. Had this been a setup?

"So what do you say, Autumn? Will you forgive me and give me another chance?"

But before Autumn could answer, Rocco took off in a run.

"Oh, no . . ." she muttered.

"Oh no?" Stanley repeated.

But she hardly heard him.

All she wanted to know was if everyone was okay.

CHAPTER THIRTY-EIGHT

GABE WATCHED as Rocco tailed the man with the gun. He'd walked by Autumn without making any moves, but it didn't mean he wasn't guilty.

In the meantime, Gabe turned back to Autumn.

Her ex wanted Autumn back. But was that all there was to it?

Based on Stanley's body language, the man was sincere. But Beckett was still researching the man's background. They couldn't take any chances.

For now, Gabe waited to see Autumn's reaction.

She licked her lips. "Stanley, I really wish you'd called me instead of coming all the way here."

"Why is that?"

"Because I'm afraid you wasted your time," Autumn said. "You had your chance with me, and you blew it. You blew it big time. There is no future for us."

Gabe let out a silent cheer. Though he'd suspected that's what Autumn would say, part of him had still been waiting on edge for confirmation.

"I really wish you would think about this," Stanley said. "We were good together, Autumn."

"I thought we were too—until I saw your true colors. You've broken my trust, and you're not ever going to get that back."

"I made a mistake." Stanley's voice hardened.

"You did. Now you have to live with those consequences. It's like I said. I wish you hadn't come here and wasted your time."

Stanley's nostrils flared. Gabe saw it from across the boardwalk. The man wasn't happy.

"Somebody called me asking about you a couple of days ago," Stanley said.

"Who was that?" Autumn's voice climbed in pitch as if she were nervous.

"He didn't give his name. He just asked where you were living now."

"Did you tell him?"

"Of course not. But he claimed you had some kind of medical benefits waiting for you from your old job. He said he needed your address so he could send you that information." Stanley paused and narrowed his eyes as he studied her. "You're not in some kind of trouble, are you?"

Gabe held his breath as he waited to see how the rest of the conversation would play out.

"I don't know why you would think that," Autumn said. "Is there a reason that I should be in trouble?"

"I guess not." Stanley shrugged.

Autumn leaned closer to him. "Is there anything you're not telling me, Stanley?"

He stared at her for a moment, his expression unreadable. "What are you talking about?"

"That's what I would like for you to tell me. Because trouble has been haunting me this week, and now here you are."

Autumn didn't pull any punches, did she? Gabe's admiration for her grew.

"I didn't come here to cause trouble," Stanley insisted. "I thought you knew me better than that."

Autumn tilted her head, her voice unwavering as she said, "How well do we really know anyone?"

AS AUTUMN STARTED BACK to the car, she sensed Gabe fall into step behind her.

At least she'd gotten that conversation with Stanley over with. But she'd hoped it would provide more answers for her. It hadn't.

Instead, their talk had only proven to uncover more hurt. As she remembered the sting of betrayal from the two people she'd at one time trusted the most, her insecurities surged to the surface.

What if she trusted Gabe only to be let down?

She hated to ask herself the question, but examining the risks was the wise thing to do. She'd been so swept away with the big emotions coming out of this situation. Having her life on the line had stirred something inside her.

Those stirrings were both good and bad. They'd helped her to realize she didn't have any time to waste. She wasn't promised tomorrow. But there was also a new urgency that called her to throw caution to the wind. When it was all over, would she still see things that way?

She wasn't sure.

She climbed into her car and locked the door. Only then did she allow herself to draw in a deep breath.

Her conversation with Stanley might be over

with, but she still needed to get back to Blackout. Plus, she wanted to know whom Rocco had been following. More had been going on back there than met the eye.

A couple of minutes later, she saw Gabe approaching and quickly opened his door. He climbed inside the car, hitting the lock behind him.

"Are you okay?" he rushed.

Autumn gripped the steering wheel but didn't take the car out of Park. "I'm fine. I guess you heard everything."

He scowled. "I did. That guy has a lot of nerve asking you to forgive him *and* take him back."

Her eyebrows shot up. "That's one way to put it. He may be clueless when it comes to love, but I don't think Stanley is involved with everything that's happened here."

"He may not be. We're still looking into his background for any possible connections, however. His presence here isn't a coincidence. Either that or he has the worst timing known to man."

Autumn shifted to better face him. "What about Rocco? What was going on with him?"

"We spotted someone suspicious—he had a gun—and we followed him, just in case."

"Did you find out anything about him?"

Gabe shook his head. "Rocco struck up a conversation with the man, and it turns out he's a state cop here on vacation with his family. Cops have a tendency to always carry their weapons with them, whether they're on duty or not."

Autumn felt her shoulders deflate just a little. Had all this been for nothing? They were leaving with no more answers than they'd come with.

Before they could talk more, Gabe's phone rang, and he excused himself to answer. But based on his expression, something else was wrong.

Autumn felt a new wave of tension thread across her chest.

What now?

CHAPTER THIRTY-NINE

GABE ENDED the call and turned to Autumn, unable to hide his unease.

"What's wrong?" she asked.

"I've been trying to get up with my friend Brandon today. I talked to him yesterday, but he hasn't been answering his phone today."

Her eyes widened as she seemed to realize the implications of what he was saying. "Do you think something happened to him?"

Gabe shrugged. "It's too early to say. I don't want to think that. But I'm getting nervous."

"Who was that who called?"

"I talked to Brandon's roommate. He said that Brandon left last night to visit his family for a couple of days. Maybe that's true, but still it doesn't make sense why he's not answering his cell phone. He's the type of guy I've always been able to reach at any time of the day or night."

"I'll be praying that your friend is okay."

"Thank you." Gabe reached for her hand and brought it to his lips. But as he pressed a soft kiss there, something changed in Autumn's gaze. He released her hand and turned to her. "What's wrong?"

She shook her head, her gaze fluttering to her lap before she glanced up nervously. "Gabe . . . I . . . I just think that maybe we should slow down."

"Slow down?" Where was this coming from? Had he misread the signals this much?

"I just mean that our emotions and adrenaline are running high right now. This is probably the worst time to start up a relationship. It's hard to know what to trust when everything seems so urgent."

He studied her face a moment, trying to read between the lines—something he'd never been good at doing. "Are you saying this in reaction to Stanley and what he put you through? Or are you saying that because it's how you really feel?"

Something flickered in her gaze. "I don't know."

At least she'd answered honestly.

"I just need a little time to think this through before I jump into something," Autumn continued. "I have so much I need to think about right now. I probably don't need any distractions."

Gabe swallowed hard. There was so much he wanted to say.

He didn't want to let her go. He wanted to remind her how good they could be together.

But he sensed that she needed space right now. Because he cared about her, he needed to give her that breathing room. She had a lot pressing on her, and he didn't want to add to that pressure.

"I understand," Gabe said. "I just want you to know that I'll be here when you finish thinking about it. You can take all the time that you want."

A smile pulled at her lips and surprise filled her gaze. "Thank you, Gabe. I appreciate it."

"Of course." He would give her some time.

Space wasn't what he wanted. He wanted to move forward. But from the start he had thought that a relationship with Autumn would be too good to be true.

Had this conversation proven him correct?

AS AUTUMN POURED over Dr. Johnson's research back at the Blackout headquarters, she sucked in a breath.

Maybe she'd been focusing on the wrong thing this whole time.

But, first, she needed to be certain before she presented her idea to anyone else.

She continued reviewing what Dr. Johnson had sent her, along with the test results from the samples that she'd taken from the four Blackout guys who'd been involved with Operation Grandiose. If this was the link she was looking for . . .

She stared at the notes and shook her head. Her idea almost sounded like a conspiracy theory—which was even more reason why she needed to make sure she knew what she was talking about before she told anyone.

But an hour later, she was nearly certain she knew what was going on.

She had an answer.

Finally.

A rumble of nerves sent a shiver through her.

She had to find Gabe. Had to tell *someone* what she had discovered.

She tore down the hallway and stopped in front of the room where the Blackout guys had gathered earlier. As she scanned the people in front of her, she spotted Gabe and Rocco. Perfect.

"I think I know what's going on." She sounded breathless to her own ears.

They both straightened and put down the papers they were looking at, their full attention on her.

"What is it?" Rocco asked.

She sat down in an empty chair and grabbed a bottle of water, taking a long sip. Then she turned to the guys. "Before you guys were deployed on any of your missions, what kind of protocols did you go through?"

"We had to have our normal battery of tests," Gabe said. "Why?"

"What about medically speaking?"

"We had to have physicals to be cleared for the task," Rocco said.

"Anything else?"

Axel leaned back in his seat. "We had to get a few inoculations."

Her mind continued to race. "What were they?"

"I couldn't tell you." Rocco shrugged. "They're so routine that I didn't even ask questions. Without them, you're sidelined for missions."

She nibbled on her bottom lip, fighting a frown.

"Is there any way you could find out what they were?"

Gabe leaned closer, his eyes narrow as he studied her face. "Do you think all this is about some kind of immunization we got?"

"It's my working theory. Based on what I saw in Dr. Johnson's research, I don't believe this is about that chemical that was sprayed on you, basically giving you each different types of autoimmune diseases."

"Why's that?"

"Without getting into too many boring details, there was an anomaly in your bloodwork that I usually see while doing the ANA test."

"The ANA test?" Gabe asked.

"It's the antinuclear antibody test—one that's given while looking for antibodies that are produced in certain autoimmune diseases. I also checked for inflammation."

"I'm still not sure I'm following," Rocco said.

"Basically, autoimmune diseases happen when the body senses danger from a virus and the immune system kicks in to attack it. Sometimes, healthy cells and tissues are caught up in the response, resulting in an autoimmune disease."

"And this goes back to our shots how?" Axel said.

"What's a vaccination?" Autumn continued. "It's usually a virus that's injected into you. There are proven cases of people getting autoimmune diseases because of them. Let me ask you this. Did any of you ever have schistosomiasis?"

"I don't even know what that is," Beckett said.

"It's an intestinal infection—from a parasite— that's fairly common in Africa. Every year, close to two hundred thousand people die from it."

"Doesn't sound familiar," Rocco said.

"I found some evidence of it in each of your bloodwork," she continued. "There have been instances in the past where military platoons have come back from sub-Sahara regions with the disease. People have been working for years on various types of vaccines for the virus."

"So you're saying that you think we were injected with something experimental?" Rocco looked tenser and tenser as the conversation went deeper.

"I do. What better guinea pigs than soldiers who have to get vaccinated before going off to do their missions?"

Silence hung in the room.

Finally, Gabe spoke again. "And you think the symptoms we're having are because of this vaccination?"

Autumn nodded, wishing she didn't have to be the one to break this news to them. "If somebody was using you as a lab rat and they realized the results were life-altering, then they might want to kill you to keep your silence rather than face the backlash over what they'd done. I think that Dr. Johnson discovered what was going on, and that's why he was killed."

The guys all exchanged glances.

"That's probably why someone's trying to kill us too." Gabe frowned. "Because we were on that mission and the proof is a part of each of us right now."

CHAPTER FORTY

GABE STEPPED onto the patio for a minute so he could have some fresh air.

He couldn't stop thinking about Autumn's theory. He hated to admit it, but her idea made sense. This could be what it was all about, and it would explain the strange symptoms each of his team members had experienced.

All along, Gabe had assumed the gas they'd been sprayed with was the culprit. But what if this went much deeper?

What if his own government was the real culprit right now? He trusted most of the people he'd worked with. But sometimes there was a bad egg in the group.

He thought about the doctor who'd given his team their shots. He had been new, someone Gabe had never worked with before.

What if the man had actually snuck something into those vaccinations and hadn't told anyone about it?

Gabe bristled with anger at the thought. He wanted to deny that somebody would go that far to do something like that. But he couldn't. He knew this was the best possibility out of all the theories that had been thrown out.

Colton was currently trying to get up with their former commander in an attempt to access their medical records and find out information on their inoculations. Gabe knew it would take time. But the more time that passed, the greater the possibility that somebody else might be hurt. That wasn't okay.

Autumn knocked at the glass door before stepping outside and joining him. When Gabe looked up and saw her, he felt something soften inside him.

He understood she'd probably been speaking from a place of fear earlier when she'd said what she had.

He really hoped Autumn would come back around. Even if she was too good for him, he still didn't want to give up hope. He'd be a fool if he did.

"Autumn . . ." He turned toward her. "What's going on?" His voice sounded more raw than he wanted.

She stepped beside him, almost looking shy. "We need answers. I've been thinking, and there's only one other person who might have them, a colleague of Dr. Johnson's named Dr. Ken Walker."

"Who is he?"

"He's the one I called when I heard about Dr. Johnson's death."

That was right . . . "You think he might provide some answers?"

Autumn shrugged. "He's the best possibility right now. The thing I'm still not clear on is how Dr. Johnson discovered this information. I know people sometimes sent him strange, 'unsolvable' cases. But I need to know some answers."

Gabe studied the determination in her gaze. "Do you think Dr. Walker might have them?"

"I don't know. But it's my best lead right now. He and Sarah, Dr. Johnson's assistant."

"You want to call them? Hear what they have to say?"

Her gaze flickered up to meet his. "Not really. I want to talk to them in person."

His throat constricted at the thought of it. "That sounds risky. Really risky."

"I know it does. But I think it's the best way. Any calls could be intercepted. Besides, I need to see Dr. Walker's eyes. I need to know what he knows."

Gabe stared at Autumn another moment and saw the resolve hardening in her gaze. Finally, he nodded. "I understand. Let me talk to Rocco and Colton and see what they say. I'll see if I can figure something out."

"Thank you." Her shoulders seemed to sag with relief.

"In the meantime, if there's any more research you need to do, now is the time. But whatever you do, please don't leave. Not without me. I need you to promise that." Gabe stared at Autumn, waiting for her reaction. He wouldn't put it past her to try to strike out on her own. He could see that passion in her.

She stared at him a moment before finally nodding. "Okay, I won't. I promise. But please don't take too long. The more time we take, the more time these guys have to plan their next move."

AUTUMN STARED out the window of the helicopter into the nighttime around her.

Blackout had somehow arranged for a friend of theirs to pick them up in the middle of the night in a copter. She and Gabe had climbed aboard and were now flying into the darkness.

Any other time, she might view something like this as an adventure. But right now, all she felt was the rising tension inside her.

She hoped this paid off, that it wasn't all for nothing. But the only people she could think of who might have answers were Dr. Walker and Sarah.

Autumn had tried to call Sarah earlier, but the woman hadn't answered, which sent another round of worry through Autumn.

So much could go wrong right now. So much.

Autumn and Gabe landed near Norfolk, where a rental car waited for them. The ride was mostly silent as they started toward Baltimore.

By the time they arrived, it should be the start of a new workday.

"You doing okay?" Gabe glanced over at her as they headed down the road.

She nodded, even though she felt uncertain. "I think so. Do you think we're being followed?"

"I don't see how." Gabe looked in the rearview mirror. "Nobody knew about our helicopter ride except for the Blackout team and our contact who owns the helicopter. Not only that, but even if someone did learn of a helicopter, they wouldn't know where we're heading. We bought ourselves a few hours, at least."

That should make Autumn feel better, but it didn't. Not really. Too much was on the line right now.

"Are you still thinking about Sarah?" Gabe's probing voice cut through the moment of quiet.

She nodded somberly. "It's bugging me that I can't get up with her. This whole situation is bugging me."

"Rightfully so."

She glanced at Gabe. "What about your friend? Brandon, right? Did you hear from him?"

As he shook his head, his jaw tightened, a give-away of his stress. "Not yet. He's a good guy, and I pray that nothing has happened to him."

"Me too. Me too." Autumn glanced at her phone.

The guys had put some kind of jammer on it so it couldn't be traced. As she checked her emails, her breath caught.

"What is it?" Gabe glanced at her.

"I just got an email from Sarah. She sent it late last night."

"What does it say?"

Autumn scanned the text before summarizing it. "She said that Dr. Johnson believed that the Dimitri family was paid to file that malpractice suit against me after Byron's death."

"Why would somebody pay them to do that?"

There was only one thing that made sense to Autumn. "Because someone wanted me to leave my job in Baltimore. Dr. Johnson believed it was so I wouldn't work with him on this project."

"Why focus on you? Why not Dr. Johnson?"

Autumn kept reading, hoping to understand everything Sarah wrote.

"She reiterated that Dr. Johnson suspected somebody was trying to get rid of him or silence him too. She believes he may have been being threatened, even though he never admitted it to her or to his wife."

"He essentially told you that in the letter he sent, right?"

"Correct." She nodded. "He clearly suspected that something might happen to him and knew that whoever he was dealing with might kill in order to keep this information silent."

"Why would someone kill to keep information silent?" Autumn felt like she already knew those answers, but she needed to talk them out.

"It usually boils down to either money, power, or love. In worst-case scenarios, it can boil down to all three."

Autumn frowned at the stark words. "Somebody stands to gain a lot of money through a new vaccine. You never heard back about what kind of shots you guys got before you left for that mission, did you?"

"Not yet. Colton is still working on that. He did find out the name of the doctor we saw. Galmarini. Does that sound familiar?"

"Unfortunately, no. I feel like we're getting so close to answers. So close." She crossed her arms over her chest, trying to comprehend the scope of what she was doing—of what she might unleash.

Maybe it was better if she didn't think about it.

She was just one person. Sure, she had Blackout on her side. But she could be going up against some giants right now, and she felt ill-prepared to handle them.

"I hope your friend might know a little bit more about what's going on here. Do you think we can trust him?"

Dr. Walker's image flashed in her mind. He was

Dr. Johnson's most trusted colleague. A former member of Doctors Without Borders. Someone who volunteered his time at a free local clinic.

"If there's anybody who can help us, it's Dr. Walker."

CHAPTER FORTY-ONE

HERE GOES NOTHING.

The phrase echoed in Gabe's mind as he stepped into the office building where Dr. Walker worked.

He watched as Autumn spoke with a woman at the front desk, and a few minutes later, they were both escorted through several sets of doors until they reached an office with Dr. Walker's nameplate out front. Inside, a fifty-something man with tan skin and dark hair greeted them.

"Autumn Spenser." He stood and grinned. "I didn't expect to see you here."

"I'm sorry to stop in unannounced."

"You're always welcome here." His gaze fell on Gabe. "And who is this?"

"This is a friend of mine, Gabe Michaels. Gabe, this is Dr. Walker."

After introductions went around, Dr. Walker grabbed a chair from his desk and carried it closer to the two other chairs against the wall.

"Please, have a seat," he instructed them.

They sat in a small circle next to each other.

"So what's going on? Is this about Dr. Johnson?" Walker's gaze latched onto Autumn's, worry filling the depths of his brown eyes.

"I wish it wasn't." Autumn rubbed her throat, almost as if she wished her muscles would loosen and that her voice wouldn't sound so tight. "I hope I'm totally out of line here and that nothing I'm about to say is true."

As Gabe listened to her statement, he knew the words were true. They were on the right track. Now there was no turning back.

"What do you need from me?" Dr. Walker laced his hands in front of him and waited.

"I'm here about Dr. Johnson's research. When you and I spoke on the phone, you had mentioned something about a project he was working on. Do you know anything about it?"

Dr. Walker shrugged, nothing registering on his

expression. "He didn't tell me anything about it. I just know he was working on something."

Autumn nodded. "I'm afraid that the implications of what he was looking into were . . . deadly."

He narrowed his eyes. "Can you explain more?"

Autumn drew in a deep breath, one appearing full of unseen burdens, before starting. "I believe Dr. Johnson discovered that somebody was developing an experimental vaccine that they were testing on members of the military. I also believe the effects of this vaccine were worse than anyone anticipated. Now, someone's trying to cover it up. They're desperate to do so, for that matter."

Dr. Walker's eyebrows shot up. "That's a big claim."

"I know. And I'm hoping that you can fill in some of the blanks." Autumn's gaze latched onto his as she drove home her point.

"What can I possibly do?"

"Do you have any idea who might be responsible for this experimental vaccine? It has to be somebody affiliated with the military doctor who was in charge of inoculating them. We believe his name is Dr. Galmarini."

Walker shook his head, his eyes slightly dazed as

if trying to process this update. "You've taken me by surprise, you've got to understand."

"I do understand. But I came here because I needed to talk to you about this face-to-face. Too many people have already been hurt. I can't risk that happening anymore."

Gabe continued to listen, hoping this trip wouldn't all be for nothing. Autumn had good instincts. She was smart. She wouldn't have wanted to do this if she didn't strongly suspect this was the best method of finding answers.

"Did Dr. Galmarini know anything?" Dr. Walker asked. "Certainly, he'd know better than anyone who could potentially be behind this."

"We're still trying to get up with him."

Walker seemed to think about what Autumn had told him for a minute before shaking his head. "I wish I could help you, Autumn, but I don't really know what to say."

Gabe bit back a frown.

Had all this been a wasted trip?

And, if so, where did they go next?

AUTUMN WATCHED as Walker shifted forward, his gaze narrowing as if he were preparing himself to ask a hard question.

He swallowed before saying, "Have you looked at Stanley?"

Autumn sucked in a breath. She hadn't expected to hear Stanley's name again. But Walker had met the man at several social events when Autumn was engaged.

She kept her voice even as she asked, "Why would you bring up Stanley?"

Walker shrugged, his motions still casual. "He *does* sell medical supplies to the military. Maybe he has some connections."

"We talked to him, but I don't believe he's guilty." She still stood behind her instincts. She hoped she wasn't wrong.

Walker let out a long breath before leaning back in his chair and staring into the distance as if in deep thought. "Stanley's the only person I can think of who might be involved. He works for a drug company. Maybe the higher-ups paid him to do something. The financial rewards might have been an incentive."

"That seems like a leap, doesn't it?" Gabe asked.

"There are plenty of people who work for the military in this area."

"But maybe that's why Stanley originally arranged for the two of you to meet. Maybe he wanted to get your feedback on what he was doing. Maybe he knew about your background. When you were dating, did he ever ask you about your work?"

Autumn's thoughts raced. She'd told Walker during a dinner at her home the story about how she'd met Stanley, so it wasn't a surprise that Dr. Walker knew those details. "Actually, Stanley did talk to me about it some."

Could Stanley really be behind this? Was his earlier explanation just a ruse?

"Maybe he's someone you need to consider then." Walker gave her a pointed look.

Autumn nodded, wondering if she'd been naive.

"Thank you for your help," she told Dr. Walker.

A strange looked crossed through Dr. Walker's gaze. He grabbed a pad from his desk and jotted something on it before holding the paper up.

THEY'RE LISTENING. **Meet me on the roof in five.**

.   .   .

HER BREATH CAUGHT.

Maybe this hadn't been a total waste of time after all.

"Please, keep me updated about what's going on," Walker said stiffly. "I want to help in whatever way I can."

Autumn nodded. "I will."

As she and Gabe left his office, her mind raced.

What did Walker really know?

CHAPTER FORTY-TWO

GABE LED Autumn from the office but didn't say anything until they reached the elevator and were out of earshot of anybody who might be listening.

"The doctor clearly thinks his office is bugged," he murmured.

"I know." Autumn shook her head. "That's not comforting."

"What do you think he knows?" Gabe asked.

"I have no idea. Maybe he has the answers we need. But it sounds like he's afraid."

"The stakes are high. He very well might be."

Gabe felt the tension coursing through him as they stopped on the eighth floor. They stepped out and found a stairway leading to the roof.

As they climbed the steps and gazed out over

downtown Baltimore, he scanned everything around them for any signs of trouble.

So far, everything looked peaceful.

Anticipation still thrummed inside him.

He glanced at his watch. It had been ten minutes.

Where was Dr. Walker?

Finally, he heard the door open and Dr. Walker stepped out.

The man nervously glanced around before joining Gabe and Autumn.

Autumn didn't waste any time getting to the point. "What do you know?"

"That you should have stayed out of it." His voice hardened.

Gabe looked down and saw the gun in the doctor's hand.

He sucked in a breath.

Dr. Walker wasn't a victim here.

He was the bad guy.

AUTUMN FELT HER LUNGS FREEZE.

"Dr. Walker?" Her voice came out in a gasp.

"You just couldn't let things go, could you?" He sneered.

"You were Dr. Johnson's friend . . ." Her mind raced. How could their colleague be behind this?

"He should have minded his own business." His words contained a bitter edge.

"How did Dr. Johnson even discover what you were doing?"

"Another doctor approached Johnson after doing some bloodwork on one of the SEALs," Walker said. "He asked Johnson to look into some anomalies. That's when he started asking too many questions. Then he realized the research I was doing was linked with the vaccine these SEALs were given before one of their missions."

"Dr. Walker . . ." Autumn's voice cracked. How could someone she'd respected so much do this?

"Now I have you two to deal with." He held up his gun again. "I hired Dagger to take care of you, but they were clearly unsuccessful."

"Why would you want to hurt so many people?" Autumn felt the tremble rake through her. "It's your job to save people . . ."

"You wouldn't understand." He raised his chin.

"So you're behind this experimental vaccine to treat schistosomiasis . . . Am I right?"

"I've been working on it for years. Ever since I lost Sylvia while she was serving with the Peace

Corps. She was the love of my life, and she left me entirely too soon."

"I'm sorry for your loss," Gabe said. "But how did your loss precipitate you testing this out on my SEAL team?"

The gun trembled in his hands. "Because you guys were the perfect subjects. You're all strong and fit. Plus, you don't have much of a choice when it comes to getting these vaccines, and you were going to the same area of the world where this runs rampant. A friend of mine helped make it happen. Dr. Galmarini."

"But things didn't turn out the way you thought, did it?" Autumn asked.

His eyes narrowed. "No one anticipated that you guys would develop autoimmune disorders as a result. Thankfully, it looked like the symptoms were from that mysterious substance sprayed on you in the heat of battle."

"How did you even know about that?" Gabe asked.

Walker's lips curled in a smile. "I have my ways."

Gabe's eyes narrowed. "When you hired Dagger, some of those guys probably told you. Most of them used to be in the military, and they must have told you about the operation."

Satisfaction glimmered in the doctor's gaze. "You put together more than I thought. Now I've got to clean up my loose ends."

Autumn's throat tightened.

How were they going to get out of this situation?

CHAPTER FORTY-THREE

GABE'S REFLEXES told him he needed to act.

But the look in Dr. Walker's eyes made it clear the man wouldn't hesitate to pull the trigger.

Gabe couldn't put Autumn in danger by making any sudden moves. Not now.

He needed to think through his next steps very carefully.

"Try anything, and I'll shoot her. Don't test me." Walker's words came out in a low growl. He must have sensed Gabe eyeing his gun.

Knowing what he now did about Dr. Walker, Gabe had no doubt the man would do just as he said. He was desperate. As Gabe had reminded Autumn earlier, desperate people did desperate things.

"Why are you doing this?" Autumn's voice trembled as she stared at his gun.

"Like I said, you weren't supposed to find out." Regret tinged Dr. Walker's words. "I'm sorry it has to be this way. I really am."

Just what was this man planning right now?

"You," he nodded to Gabe before pointing with his gun, "step closer to the edge of the building."

Gabe felt himself tense.

He'd been forced to leave his own gun in the car because of the metal detectors at the front door of the building. Otherwise, he felt certain he would have been able draw it quickly enough to take the doctor down.

Gabe had to play it safe here in order for Autumn not to be hurt.

For that reason, he followed Walker's orders and took a few steps back. A twelve-inch-high brick ledge lined the perimeter of the roof.

Gabe didn't have to look to know it was a long way down.

He knew he could take Dr. Walker on. Knew that he was stronger.

But he couldn't risk Autumn being in the crossfire.

As soon as Gabe stepped back, Dr. Walker

wrapped an arm around Autumn's throat and jerked her back against himself. He put his gun back into his pocket and pulled out something else.

A . . . needle.

Gabe's throat went dry.

What was inside that syringe?

FROM AUTUMN'S PERIPHERAL VISION, she saw the needle emerge and sucked in a breath.

"What's in that?" Part of her didn't want to know.

"I've been working on improving the vaccine that I developed," Walker hissed. "I'd like you to be my test subject now."

Autumn's entire body tensed. "So what are you going to do? Inject me, then hold me captive until you see how my body reacts? That doesn't seem like a great plan."

"I tried to test it on Sarah last night, but, unfortunately, she had a terrible reaction. Blood clots."

"What?" Disbelief stretched through Autumn's voice. "You didn't . . ."

Then again, if Walker had killed Dr. Johnson, there was no telling what he might do.

"I was able to cover my tracks so the police and

medical examiner won't get suspicious. It simply looks like she overdosed. I even had her write a note saying how she was mourning Dr. Johnson's death and couldn't handle life anymore. It's been a very busy day, to say the least."

"You're despicable," Autumn muttered. He disgusted her. How could she have admired this man at one time?

"I didn't want it to be this way, but I don't have any other choice."

"What about Gabe?" Autumn glanced at him as he stood near the edge of the roof. "You inject me and wait for the vaccine to take effect. Then what are you going to do with him?"

"You don't need to worry about that. You'll have your own issues to focus on."

"Don't do it." Tension thrummed through Gabe's voice.

"Why not?"

"Why don't you use me instead?" Gabe held out his arm, volunteering to be a test subject instead of Autumn.

"Gabe . . ." Autumn's heart pounded in her ears. That wasn't what she wanted. She needed to know Gabe was going to be okay.

Gabe's gaze locked with hers. "You know I'd do anything for you, Autumn."

As his words washed over her, she realized they were the truth. She'd be a fool to ever let someone like Gabe walk out of her life. He was *nothing* like Stanley. He was constantly putting Autumn above himself.

But would she ever have the chance to tell him that?

As she felt the needle begin to prick her arm, she realized she had her answer.

CHAPTER FORTY-FOUR

GABE SAW the needle poking into Autumn's skin and knew he had to act.

Without wasting any more time, he dove toward the doctor.

He tackled the man onto the ground. As he did, Autumn staggered backward, away from the struggle. The gun fell from Walker's pocket and slid across the concrete away from them.

As Gabe looked at the man's other hand, he spotted the syringe, which had been jerked from Autumn's arm during the scuffle.

Walker raised his hand, trying to jab the needle into Gabe.

Before he could, Gabe pressed the doctor's arm into the ground.

The man fought back, stronger than Gabe expected.

Autumn let out a scream beside them before kicking the syringe from Walker's hand.

The needle flew out of reach across the rooftop. As it did, Autumn reached down and grabbed Walker's gun. With trembling hands, she raised it.

Gabe didn't want her to have to use it. He just needed a few more seconds . . .

Gabe slammed Walker's arm into the ground again. Finally, the man stopped struggling and collapsed against the ground, nearly limp with resignation.

"I never meant for any of this to happen." His voice cracked. "I just didn't want anyone else suffer like my Sylvia did."

"Yet you made me and my friends suffer," Gabe muttered, still pinning him down.

"I didn't mean to. The FDA wouldn't approve it, even after I spent ten years of my life developing it, and . . . I had to take action on my own. My work was valuable. It could change lives."

"I'm sure it was." Autumn shook her head as she stared down at him. She'd lowered the gun but still held it, probably just in case they had any more surprises. "But there's a right and a wrong way to go about it. You should know that."

Before Walker could respond, police flooded the rooftop.

Gabe didn't know who had called the cops, but he was glad they did.

Maybe this was finally over.

Maybe.

AFTER AUTUMN FINISHED GIVING her state-ment to the police, her gaze scanned everyone until she found Gabe. They were still gathered on the roof as law enforcement collected evidence.

As she glanced at Gabe, a rush of gratitude swept through her. There was so much she wanted to say to him.

And she would . . . soon.

Right now, they had other things to take care of.

It turned out that Rocco had discovered Dr. Walker was associated with Dr. Galmarini. When he'd tried to contact Gabe to warn him, Gabe hadn't answered his phone.

Rocco had immediately called in backup.

Law enforcement officers had arrived on scene

and intercepted Dagger agents who'd shown up and were about to breach the building.

Arrests had been made, and this ordeal finally appeared to be over.

When the police finally dismissed them, Gabe joined Autumn. The tenderness in his eyes made her heart do cartwheels—as did his earlier selflessness. She would be a fool to let someone like him go.

"Are you okay?" he murmured.

She nodded. "I am. Thanks to you. The needle pricked my arm, but he wasn't able to inject me with anything."

"I would have taken the shot for you, you know. One from the needle or the gun."

Warmth flooded her chest. "I know you would have, Gabe. Thank you."

"I'm so glad you're okay." Gabe's voice sounded throaty with emotion as he stared at her.

The next instant, Autumn threw her arms around his neck. He stiffened before wrapping his arms around her waist and pulling her close. "What's this for?"

"Gabe . . ." How did she even say this? "I want to give us a try."

He pulled back until their gazes connected. "You do? But I thought . . . ?"

"I'd be a fool to ever let someone like you get away. Seeing Stanley again brought back so many bad memories and—"

"I get it."

"You were willing to sacrifice yourself for me." Autumn rubbed her lips together. "When I realized that, it did something to my heart. I realized . . ." She struggled to find the right words to say.

"You realized . . ."

"How much I care about you," she blurted.

She held her breath as she waited for his reaction.

He stared at her a moment before a grin slowly stretched across his face. "You have no idea how happy it makes me to hear you say that."

A gush of relief—and joy—flooded Autumn.

He leaned toward her, and their lips met.

EPILOGUE

"I SAY there's no better time for sushi than now." Rocco raised his chopsticks, proudly displaying the volcano roll on the end.

"Hear, hear!" Beckett raised his own sushi—a spicy tuna roll.

The four recruits pretended to clank their sushi together in a cheer as they sat around a table inside Peyton's Pastries.

Peyton had generously offered to make them the treat as a celebration. In fact, she'd been perfecting her skills over the past few weeks, just so she could surprise the Blackout members. Lisa had worked with her and they'd even developed a few unique combinations, including a bacon and egg sushi— using the crispy bacon as the wrapper.

Now that doctors knew what had caused the team's ailments, medical professionals would be able to better treat them. Progress could be made. They could each move on.

Even though they'd been through a storm to get to this point, at least they were now on the upside of things. And part of that was because of the work Autumn had done in finding answers.

Dr. Walker had been arrested, along with Dr. Galmarini. Dagger had been shut down, and three operatives had been arrested. Those guys—including Max—had been behind the events here on Lantern Beach, including leaving that black mamba in Gabe's car.

It turned out that it wasn't just Gabe's SEAL team that had been used for the experimental vaccine. Other military members had also been test subjects.

An intensive investigation and lawsuit were currently in progress.

Their friend, Brandon, had been found. He'd been carjacked while working at the auto dealership. He'd fought off his assailants, but they'd left him beaten on the side of a deserted road. Thankfully, he was doing okay.

Gabe glanced around the table. Rocco and Peyton smiled at each other. Axel and Olivia spoke in quiet tones. Beckett and Sami shared some kind of inside joke as they both grabbed another sushi roll from the platter at the center of the table.

As the door to Peyton's Pastries opened, Gabe sucked in a breath.

Autumn stepped inside, and her gaze found his. A smile lit her face.

In three strides, Gabe crossed the room and met her. He had hoped she would be able to get off work in time to come.

But before he could say anything, his gaze went to her shirt. He sucked in a breath as memories filled him.

"Nice shirt," he muttered.

She glanced down and grinned. "I think this makes me an official Lantern Beach resident. Isn't that what you said?"

He smiled, vaguely remembering that conversation from their first encounter at the beginning of this mess. "It does."

"You stopped by to bring me this shirt that night, didn't you? I found it outside the other day. It had fallen between the steps and some bushes. At first, I didn't understand. Then I remembered our conversation from that day I treated you in the clinic."

He shrugged, trying to play it off. "What if I did?"

"Why didn't you tell me?" She studied his expression.

"We had a lot going on. It didn't seem important."

"But it *was* important," she told him. "It just took me a while to put things together."

Gabe reached for her waist. "What can I say? I just wanted to let you know that you are an official part of things around here."

She grinned. "I'm glad to hear that."

He stared into her eyes, wanting nothing more than to reach down and kiss her. But not here. Not now.

There would be time for that later.

Instead, he turned back to his friends at the table. "Peyton just pulled out the sushi."

She glanced beyond him at the group at the table. They all called their hellos to her.

Autumn turned back to him. "It sounds like you guys deserve a little celebration."

"We wouldn't be celebrating if it weren't for you." He hoped she heard the sincerity in his voice.

"I don't know about that . . . you guys would have figured things out." She reached down and squeezed his hand. "I have faith in you."

Hearing her affirmations never got old. Gabe

brought her hand to his lips and planted a kiss there. "Thank you, Autumn."

"You're welcome, Gabe." A teasing tone filled her voice. "By the way, how do you feel about having dinner with Doc Clemson and Ernestine? Doc volunteered to make his blackberry pie."

Gabe raised his eyebrows. "Blackberry pie? I'm in."

"Just for the pie?"

He leaned closer. "With you, I'm always in. Just say the word."

He meant it. Now that he'd found Autumn, he couldn't imagine his future without her. He hoped she felt the same way.

They shared another smile before turning back to the team.

Now, it was time to celebrate.

"Hey, let's talk about who won that bet," Rocco called. "Autumn, when exactly did he ask you out and are you sure you said yes?"

Another round of laughter went around the table.

~~~

Thank you for reading *Gabe*. If you enjoyed this book, I'd love a review! Stay tuned for Lantern Beach Blackout: Danger Rising, a new series coming 2022.

COMING 2022: BRANDON

LANTERN BEACH MYSTERIES

Hidden Currents

You can take the detective out of the investigation, but you can't take the investigator out of the detective. A notorious gang puts a bounty on Detective Cady Matthews's head after she takes down their leader, leaving her no choice but to hide until she can testify at trial. But her temporary home across the country on a remote North Carolina island isn't as peaceful as she initially thinks. Living under the new identity of Cassidy Livingston, she struggles to keep her investigative skills tucked away, especially after a body washes ashore. When local police bungle the murder investigation, she can't resist stepping in. But

Cassidy is supposed to be keeping a low profile. One wrong move could lead to both her discovery and her demise. Can she bring justice to the island . . . or will the hidden currents surrounding her pull her under for good?

Flood Watch

The tide is high, and so is the danger on Lantern Beach. Still in hiding after infiltrating a dangerous gang, Cassidy Livingston just has to make it a few more months before she can testify at trial and resume her old life. But trouble keeps finding her, and Cassidy is pulled into a local investigation after a man mysteriously disappears from the island she now calls home. A recurring nightmare from her time undercover only muddies things, as does a visit from the parents of her handsome ex-Navy SEAL neighbor. When a friend's life is threatened, Cassidy must make choices that put her on the verge of blowing her cover. With a flood watch on her emotions and her life in a tangle, will Cassidy find the truth? Or will her past finally drown her?

Storm Surge

A storm is brewing hundreds of miles away, but its effects are devastating even from afar. Laid-back, loose, and light: that's Cassidy Livingston's new motto. But when a makeshift boat with a bloody cloth inside washes ashore near her oceanfront home, her detective instincts shift into gear . . . again. Seeking clues isn't the only thing on her mind—romance is heating up with next-door neighbor and former Navy SEAL Ty Chambers as well. Her heart wants the love and stability she's longed for her entire life. But her hidden identity only leads to a tidal wave of turbulence. As more answers emerge about the boat, the danger around her rises, creating a treacherous swell that threatens to reveal her past. Can Cassidy mind her own business, or will the storm surge of violence and corruption that has washed ashore on Lantern Beach leave her life in wreckage?

Dangerous Waters

Danger lurks on the horizon, leaving only two choices: find shelter or flee. Cassidy Livingston's new identity has begun to feel as comfortable as her favorite sweater. She's been tucked away on Lantern Beach for weeks, waiting to testify against a deadly gang, and is settling in to a new life she wants to last forever. When she thinks she spots someone malevolent from her past, panic swells inside her. If an enemy has found her, Cassidy won't be the only one who's a target. Everyone she's come to love will also be at risk. Dangerous waters threaten to pull her into an overpowering chasm she may never escape. Can Cassidy survive what lies ahead? Or has the tide fatally turned against her?

Perilous Riptide

Just when the current seems safer, an unseen danger emerges and threatens to destroy everything. When Cassidy Livingston finds a journal hidden deep in the recesses of her ice cream truck, her curiosity kicks into high gear. Islanders suspect that Elsa, the journal's owner, didn't die accidentally. Her final entry indicates their suspicions might be correct and that what Elsa observed on her final night may have led to her demise. Against the advice of Ty Chambers, her former Navy SEAL boyfriend, Cassidy taps into her detective skills and hunts for answers. But her search only leads to a skeletal body and trouble for both of them. As helplessness threatens to drown her, Cassidy is desperate to turn back time. Can Cassidy find what she needs to navigate the perilous situation? Or will the riptide surrounding her threaten everyone and everything Cassidy loves?

Deadly Undertow

The current's fatal pull is powerful, but so is one detective's will to live. When someone from Cassidy Livingston's past shows up on Lantern Beach and warns her of impending peril, opposing currents collide, threatening to drag her under. Running would be easy. But leaving would break her heart. Cassidy must decipher between the truth and lies, between reality and deception. Even more importantly, she must decide whom to trust and whom to fear. Her life depends on it. As danger rises and answers surface, everything Cassidy thought she knew is tested. In order to survive, Cassidy must take drastic measures and end the battle against the ruthless gang DH-7 once and for all. But if her final mission fails, the consequences will be as deadly as the raging undertow.

LANTERN BEACH ROMANTIC SUSPENSE

Tides of Deception

Change has come to Lantern Beach: a new police chief, a new season, and . . . a new romance? Austin Brooks has loved Skye Lavinia from the moment they met, but the walls she keeps around her seem impenetrable. Skye knows Austin is the best thing to ever happen to her. Yet she also knows that if he learns the truth about her past, he'd be a fool not to run. A chance encounter brings secrets bubbling to the surface, and danger soon follows. Are the life-threatening events plaguing them really accidents . . . or is someone trying to send a deadly message? With the tides on Lantern Beach come deception and lies. One question remains—who will be swept away as the water shifts? And will it bring the end for Austin and Skye, or merely the beginning?

Shadow of Intrigue

For her entire life, Lisa Garth has felt like a supporting character in the drama of life. The designation never bothered her—until now. Lantern Beach, where she's settled and runs a popular restaurant, has boarded up for the season. The slower pace leaves her with too much time alone. Braden Dillinger came to Lantern Beach to try to heal. The former Special Forces officer returned from battle with invisible scars and diminished hope. But his recovery is hampered by the fact that an unknown enemy is trying to kill him. From the moment Lisa and Braden meet, danger ignites around them, and both are drawn into a web of intrigue that turns their lives upside down. As shadows creep in, will Lisa and Braden be able to shine a light on the peril around them? Or will the encroaching darkness turn their worst nightmares into reality?

Storm of Doubt

A pastor who's lost faith in God. A romance writer who's lost faith in love. A faceless man with a deadly obsession. Nothing has felt right in Pastor Jack Wilson's world since his wife died two years ago. He hoped coming to Lantern Beach might help soothe the ragged edges of his soul. Instead, he feels more alone than ever. Novelist Juliette Grace came to the island to hide away. Though her professional life has never been better, her personal life has imploded. Her husband left her and a stalker's threats have grown more and more dangerous. When Jack saves Juliette from an attack, he sees the terror in her gaze and knows he must protect her. But when danger strikes again, will Jack be able to keep her safe? Or will the approaching storm prove too strong to withstand?

Winds of Danger

Wes O'Neill is perfectly content to hang with his friends and enjoy island life on Lantern Beach.

Something begins to change inside him when Paige Henderson sweeps into his life. But the beautiful newcomer is hiding painful secrets beneath her cheerful facade. Police dispatcher Paige Henderson came to Lantern Beach riddled with guilt and uncertainties after the fallout of a bad relationship. When she meets Wes, she begins to open up to the possibility of love again. But there's something Wes isn't telling her—something that could change everything. As the winds shift, doubts seep into Paige's mind. Can Paige and Wes trust each other, even as the currents work against them? Or is trouble from the past too much to overcome?

Rains of Remorse

A stranger invades her home, leaving Rebecca Jarvis terrified. Above all, she must protect the baby growing inside her. Since her estranged husband died suspiciously six months earlier, Rebecca has been determined to depend on no one but herself. Her chivalrous new neighbor appears to be an answer to prayer. But who is Levi Stoneman really? Rebecca wants to believe he can help her, but she can't ignore her instincts. As danger closes in, both Rebecca and Levi must figure out whom they can trust. With Rebecca's baby coming soon, there's no time to waste. Can the truth prevail . . . or will remorse overpower the best of intentions?

Torrents of Fear

The woman lingering in the crowd can't be Allison . . . can she? Because Allison was pronounced dead six years ago. Musician Carter Denver knows only one person who's capable of helping him find answers: Sadie Thompson, his estranged best friend and someone who also knew Allison. He needs to know if he's losing his mind or if Allison could have survived her car accident. Could Allison really be alive? If so, why is she trying to harm Carter and Sadie? As the two try to find answers, can Sadie keep her feelings for Carter hidden? Could he ever care for her, or is the man of her dreams still in love with the woman now causing his nightmares?

LANTERN BEACH PD

On the Lookout

When Cassidy Chambers accepted the job as police chief on Lantern Beach, she knew the island had its secrets. But a suspicious death with potentially far-reaching implications will test all her skills

—and threaten to reveal her true identity. Cassidy enlists the help of her husband, former Navy SEAL Ty Chambers. As they dig for answers, both uncover parts of their pasts that are best left buried. Not everything is as it seems, and they must figure out if their John Doe is connected to the secretive group that has moved onto the island. As facts materialize, danger on the island grows. Can Cassidy and Ty discover the truth about the shadowy crimes in their cozy community? Or has darkness permanently invaded their beloved Lantern Beach?

Attempt to Locate

A fun girls' night out turns into a nightmare when armed robbers barge into the store where Cassidy and her friends are shopping. As the situation escalates and the men escape, a massive manhunt launches on Lantern Beach to apprehend the dangerous trio. In the midst of the chaos, a potential foe asks for Cassidy's help. He needs to find his sister who fled from the secretive Gilead's Cove community on the island. But the more Cassidy learns about the seemingly untouchable group, the more her unease grows. The pressure to solve both cases continues to mount. But as the gravity of the situation rises, so does the danger. Cassidy is determined to protect the island and break up the cult . . . but doing so might cost her everything.

First Degree Murder

Police Chief Cassidy Chambers longs for a break from the recent crimes plaguing Lantern Beach. She simply wants to enjoy her friends' upcoming wedding, to prepare for the busy tourist season about to slam the island, and to gather all the dirt she can on the suspicious community that's invaded the town. But trouble explodes on the island, sending residents—including Cassidy—into a squall of uneasiness. Cassidy may have more than one enemy plotting her demise, and the collateral damage seems unthinkable. As the temperature rises, so does the pressure to find answers. Someone is determined that Lantern Beach would be better off without their new police chief. And for Cassidy, one wrong move could mean certain death.

Dead on Arrival

With a highly charged local election consuming the community, Police Chief Cassidy Chambers braces herself for a challenging day of breaking up petty conflicts and tamping down high emotions. But when widespread food poisoning spreads among potential voters across the island, Cassidy smells something rotten in the air. As Cassidy examines every possibility to uncover what's going on, local enigma Anthony Gilead again comes on her radar. The man is running for mayor and his cult-like following is growing at an alarming rate. Cassidy feels certain he has a spy embedded in her inner circle. The problem is that her pool of suspects gets deeper every day. Can Cassidy get to the bottom of what's eating away at her peaceful island home? Will voters turn out despite the outbreak of illness plaguing their tranquil town? And the even bigger question: Has darkness come to stay on Lantern Beach?

Plan of Action

A missing Navy SEAL. Danger at the boiling point. The ultimate showdown. When Police Chief Cassidy Chambers' husband, Ty, disappears, her world is turned upside down. His truck is discovered with blood inside, crashed in a ditch on Lantern Beach, but he's nowhere to be found. As they launch a manhunt to find him, Cassidy discovers that someone on the island has a deadly obsession with Ty. Meanwhile, Gilead's Cove seems to be imploding. As danger heightens, federal law enforcement officials are called in. The cult's growing threat could lead to the pinnacle standoff of good versus evil. A clear plan of action is needed or the results will be devastating. Will Cassidy find Ty in time, or will she face a gut-wrenching loss? Will Anthony Gilead finally be unmasked for who he really is and be brought to justice? Hundreds of innocent lives are at stake . . . and not everyone will come out alive.

LANTERN BEACH BLACKOUT

Dark Water

Colton Locke can't forget the black op that went terribly wrong. Desperate for a new start, he moves to Lantern Beach, North Carolina, and forms Blackout, a private security firm. Despite his hero status, he can't erase the mistakes he's made. For the past year, Elise Oliver hasn't been able to shake the feeling that there's more to her husband's death than she was told. When she finds a hidden box of his personal possessions, more questions—and suspicions—arise. The only person she trusts to help her is her husband's best friend, Colton Locke. Someone wants Elise dead. Is it because she knows too much? Or is it to keep her from finding the truth? The Blackout team must uncover dark secrets hiding beneath seemingly still waters. But those very secrets might just tear the team apart.

Safe Harbor

Guilt over past mistakes haunts former Navy SEAL Dez Rodriguez. When he's asked to guard a pop star during a music festival on Lantern Beach, he's all set for what he hopes is a breezy assignment. Bree hasn't found fame to be nearly as fulfilling as she dreamed. Instead, she's more like a carefully crafted character living out a pre-scripted story. When a stalker's threats become deadly, her life—and career—are turned upside down. From the start, Bree sees her temporary bodyguard as a player, and Dez sees Bree as a spoiled rich girl. But when they're thrown together in a fight for survival, both must learn to trust. Can Dez protect Bree—and his carefully guarded heart? Or will their safe harbor ultimately become their death trap?

Ripple Effect

Griff McIntyre never expected his ex-wife and three-year-old daughter to come to Lantern Beach. After an abduction attempt, they're desperate for safety. Now Griff's not letting either of them out of his sight. Bethany knows Griff is the only one who can protect them, despite the fact that he broke her heart. But she'll do anything to keep her daughter safe—even if it means playing nicely with a man she can't stand. As peril ripples through their lives, Griff and Bethany must work together to protect their daughter. But an unseen enemy wants something from them . . . and will stop at nothing to get it. When disaster strikes, can Griff keep his family safe? Or will past mistakes bring the ultimate failure?

Rising Tide

Benjamin James knows there's a traitor within his former command. The rest of his team might even think it's him. As danger closes in, he must clear himself and stop a deadly plot by a dangerous terrorist group. All CJ Compton wanted was a new start after her career ended under suspicion. Working as the house manager for private security group Blackout seems perfect. But there's more trouble here than what she left behind. As the tide rushes in, the stakes continue to rise. If the Blackout team fails, it's not just Lantern Beach at stake—it's the whole country. Can Benjamin and CJ overcome their differences and work together to find the truth?

ABOUT THE AUTHOR

USA Today has called Christy Barritt's books "scary, funny, passionate, and quirky."

Christy writes both mystery and romantic suspense novels that are clean with underlying messages of faith. Her books have won the Daphne du Maurier Award for Excellence in Suspense and Mystery, have been twice nominated for the Romantic Times Reviewers' Choice Award, and have finaled for both a Carol Award and Foreword Magazine's Book of the Year.

She is married to her Prince Charming, a man who thinks she's hilarious—but only when she's not trying to be. Christy is a self-proclaimed klutz, an avid music lover who's known for spontaneously bursting into song, and a road trip aficionado.

When she's not working or spending time with her family, she enjoys singing, playing the guitar, and exploring small, unsuspecting towns where people have no idea how accident-prone she is.

Find Christy online at:
    www.christybarritt.com
    www.facebook.com/christybarritt
    www.twitter.com/cbarritt

Sign up for Christy's newsletter to get information on all of her latest releases here: **www. christybarritt.com/newsletter-sign-up/**

If you enjoyed this book, please consider leaving a review.

10447239R00215